Put It In The Bag Publishing Presents

Murder Bout Money

By: J. Latimer

ISBN: 9798834816430

Printed in the USA

In Loving memory of Jaylen AKA Little JLab
Forever in our hearts

Murder Bout Money

It's hard to smile when you come from the gutter for real,
you can't imagine the daily experiences of my life—
It's like ichthyology with niggas…
So yes, we murder 'bout money, not women.
This cold world keeps me and my villains wearing ice…
When them guns come out, let the record reflect,
you should pay what you owe,
because we Murder Bout Money.
Walk with the hustlers,
Eat with the grinders,
Party with the bosses.
It's all about the money, Cuz,
All my niggas "rollin"', get it????

Murder Bout Money

This is a work of fiction. All the characters, organizations, and events portrayed in this novel are either products of the author's imagination or are used fictitiously.

Designed by Deshonda Oden.

CHAPTER 1

MURDER BOUT MONEY

Shots rang out in a busy Hawkins Plaza parking lot at about two p.m. Two young, Black males laid lifeless, bloody with shopping bags scattered around them, and people rushed out of stores to get a better look.

Keyshore jumped back into the rental car he was driving and hauled ass down V. Odom Blvd.

He felt no remorse for the life of his younger cousin Demond, or the dude with him. The only thing that upset him was he knew he would have to pay for the funeral and lie about what he did.

His cousin Demond did this to himself—he ran off with ten pounds of ice and three grams of Fentanyl that took a thousand (meaning that he turned it into three thousand grams).

Keyshore had been looking for Demond going

on a year, so he knew his cousin had no intentions to pay him back. His little cousin bragged and boasted on social media, flaunting money, jewels, and Rolex watches, but refused to answer any of his calls.

Little did Demond know that while he was spending big money on clothes and shoes, one of Keyshore's bitches worked at that store. "Murder 'Bout Money" was the code in the streets, and Keyshore stood on that belief—and so did everybody in his circle.

NBA YoungBoy played in Keyshore's truck when he switched vehicles with Lil' Mark, who took the rental car and burnt it up.

Back at the crime scene, police and homicide detectives circled around the two victims. Yellow tape blocked off the store to the parking lot, where shell casings laid all around.

Detective Anderson spoke loud and clear, "This looks like a vengeful killing... whoever did this was very upset and determined!"

All the officers nodded their heads in agreement.

Neither of the two young victims carried any ID, so until their fingerprints came back, the officers had no clue who they were.

Two female officers took notes as they questioned two witnesses who couldn't seem to identify the killer. The shooter fired so many shots that by the time he stopped, and people came up from covering, he was long gone.

Detective Anderson was furious that nobody knew shit about a double homicide that happened in broad daylight. By the time he left the crime scene, it was dark. He headed to the station to see if the identities of the victims came in yet.

When fingerprints came back, the results showed the victims were Demond Williams, age twenty-six, and Bill Lewis, age twenty-two.

Detective Anderson quickly jumped on his computer. To his surprise, Bill Lewis had an outstanding warrant for murder in Middletown, Ohio, and a federal warrant for an overdose. Demond Williams' name had just popped up in a federal conspiracy wire-tap, and a warrant had just been signed a day before his murder.

The Detective shook his head. Something fishy was in the air, and like a bloodhound, he was going to sniff it out.

He got up out his chair and screamed for his phone officer to notify the families of the victims. Although he could care less about their deaths, it was his job.

When Demond's mother got the news, she fell to the floor in pain. Demond was her only child that had made it—even though it wasn't legit. He always made sure his mother was well off; he paid her rent and all her bills every month. She prayed it wasn't her son, because no one knew for sure yet, but deep down. She knew once they gave details of the necklace found on one of the victim's necks.

Keyshore hung up the phone with his crying aunt and headed towards her house. When he arrived, all his aunt's children and their kids sat, gathered around the house in tears.

Keyshore hugged his aunt first, then his two girl cousins, and then their brother. He then picked up his girl cousin's son, Lil' ' Matt, when his Aunt Sandy signaled for him to come in a separate room to speak with her privately.

With tears in her eyes, she spoke quietly.

"I know Demond looked up to you dearly… and you've done a lot for him. I—… I know he would want you to have this more than anyone else."

Sandy reached in the closet, and her hand reappeared with a large Gucci book bag. She handed it to Keyshore and told him she didn't know what all was in it, but she knew it was drugs, if anything.

Keyshore sat Lil' ' Matt down and he quickly ran out of the room and into the living room with his mother. When Keyshore unzipped the bag, stacks of money appeared. He dumped it all out on the floor.

"No drugs in here," he spoke to his aunt.

Keyshore closed the room door, then began counting the money—which didn't take long, because it was in stacks of 10K each. He cursed Demond out in his head. Greed cost his cousin his life; Demond had *over* the amount he owed Keyshore.

Keyshore took half—which was about 20K over the amount owed to him—and told his aunt she should keep the rest.

If only his aunt knew she was looking in the face of her son's killer...

CHAPTER 2

The Good Die Young

The new crack was ice—better known as "crystal meth." With Covid-19 shutting down the world, people were forced to run around with masks on their face.

Nothing stopped the business, though; Keyshore and Lil' ' Mark had an icehouse in Kenmore that was doing numbers. All day long, traffic came and went.

***

Although Keyshore never spoke about killing his little cousin, Mark knew it bothered him. Lil' Mark still couldn't believe that Keyshore had the nuts to even attend Demond's funeral, knowing he was the cause of his death. But he did, front and center, like Bishop in the movie "*Juice.*" The only difference - this wasn't a movie.

The funeral was truly sad. With the Covid-19 virus being so deadly, people couldn't crowd the building where Demond's body was held. Outside, people stood around in tears with their masks on.

Just to be safe, the pastor did the ceremony outside.

The man was loved dearly. He packed Thornton Street with so many people, and cars blocked off the roads all the way from Lane Street to Manchester Road. People smoked weed, drank bottles, and cheered Demond's name with love and tears.

Loud music played from so many different car systems, and women shook their asses. It was like a block party. It got so bad that they had to bury Demond the next day because the police couldn't get people to make way for the hearse and limousine to leave.

After Demond was laid to rest, life went on, and so did the game. He was just a memory.

A dude named Jim from his 'hood started fucking his girl, and two weeks later, Jim was wearing all his old clothes and even driving the car Demond had bought her.

Lil' Mark was even creeping with the girl, getting his dick sucked for thirty perky pills. The game was the game, and survival was key.

***

Keyshore pulled into Sam's Corner store on V. Odom Boulevard. Old dope-fiends he knew from when he was a kid hung around the store, asking for change to buy beer.

Today, Keyshore was feeling good, so he gave everyone five bucks each, then entered the store to buy a gyro. After he paid for his food and purchased a few single cigarettes, he headed back outside to smoke until his food was ready.

Just having Keyshore in the presence packed the store up real quick. Cars started pulling up left and right to holler at Keyshore while he stood outside. Sam loved when he came because his business always picked up good.

Keyshore stood in front of the store, laughing, and talking to a few girls and a couple of his ‘hood niggas. His homeboy, Nard, cracked jokes on how cheap Keyshore was, and the fact that he always bought single cigarettes instead of a pack with all the money he had.

Just then, the S.N.U.D. police hit the corner of Ramon St. and V. Odom, looking hard at all the activity at Sam's store.

Everyone continued laughing and carrying on, but Keyshore locked eyes with one of the racist, white police officers. He shook his head; it didn't make any sense to him how they sent racist police to the black community.

The police circled the block a few times more, then went on their way. With all the Black Lives Matter movements and senseless police killings on the blacks, the racist cops were given warnings not to harass them. As bad as they wanted to jump out and search all the niggers for drugs and guns, they had no probable cause.

Life in Akron, Ohio was something else. Who would think a city so small would be as fast as it was? There was no "*First 48*" TV show here; People were killed left and right, and nobody went to jail for it.

Detective Anderson was in the hot seat ever since one of LeBron James' close friends got killed, and that murder was still unsolved.

CHAPTER 3

Hembra Pasillo

Joy sped up Archwood in her red 2019 Dodge Charger with black limo tint. When she got close to the corner of Arlington, she noticed her little homie, Young Ruler standing out front of the drive thru. She couldn't believe her eyes—this nigga really thought she was a joke.

Joy continued, turning left on Arlington, and heading to 5th Ave.

Young Ruler, who everyone had love for on the east side, turned sixteen years old today. Although he had been laying low ever since he chalked his blood homie's girl Joy, he wasn't going to continue to hide from a bitch, and his dude LX—which was *her* dude—was up the road serving ten years on a drug charge.

Young Ruler stood outside the drive thru with

all his young niggas, and best believe everyone was strapped. They smoked blunt after blunt and sipped on a fifth of XO. When the red Charger passed by, Ruler caught a funny vibe.

He asked his boy Red Dawg, “Whose car was that?”

Red Dawg didn't have a clue—so many cars drove up and down their strip, he couldn't keep track.

One thing Young Ruler made sure of was that all his boys were on their feet when he chalked Joy. Just knowing they all had guns and were with him eased his mind.

***

Joy sped all the way down 5th Ave until she came upon the dead-end part. She left her car running while she jumped out and ran into the trap house to grab her gun. When she entered, little Zeek noticed the rage in her eyes as she rushed past him.

Joy wasn't your regular woman. Her beauty fooled a lot of people, but this girl was only nineteen years old and had already claimed the lives of a few people.

Little did she know that Young Ruler was really cool with gold-digging Ida, who happened to stay next door.

Ida phoned Ruler the minute she saw Joy jump out of her car. She gave him the whole run-down.

Zeek stopped Joy before she left. He warned her about Ruler, and how he even spotted him next door.

Joy took a mental note, then proceded out the door back into her car.

As she was pulling in the driveway to back out, she noticed someone peeking out of Ida's curtains. She played it off like she didn't notice.

When Joy returned up on Archwood, Young Ruler and his crew were nowhere to be found.

She pulled back on 5th Ave, and this time, she decided to park at Rocky's store and creep down on Ida.

The timing was perfect.

While Joy walked up with her red hoodie tied tight over her face, Ida had just buckled her last child out of three into her car seat.

As soon as she closed the door and turned around to get in the driver seat, Joy shot her in the face, point-blank range, then ran through the cut.

Little Zeek clutched for his gun when he heard the loud gunshot outside. When he pulled the curtain back to look outside, he saw Ida laid out with blood gushing from her head. The kids in the car screamed in fear and people began to run out of numerous houses to the crime scene.

Zeek shook his head—he knew Joy and how she got down.

When Young Ruler got the news about Ida, he broke down in tears. He knew he was the cause. Ida saved his life, but lost her own.

"This turned out to be the worst birthday ever," Ruler thought as he passed six corners, heading to Eastland woods. Shit got real fast, and now he wished he'd paid Joy her money.

Ruler pulled into his in-home garage, then entered his auntie's house. She never stayed there, so it was more like his own home. Plus, he paid all the bills. The rent wasn't much, because it was Section 8 housing.

He took a long, hot shower then played some video games alone. He didn't trust many people, and the only reason he went to his 'hood was because it was his birthday.

***

The next day after Joy killed Ida, she headed to the West side to meet up with Keyshore for business. Today, Keyshore had her coming to Kenmore—she usually met him at the barbershop on V. Odom.

Keyshore and Lil' Mark sat on the porch as Joy parked on the curve. Joy got out of the rental truck she had been driving, looking very beautiful. Although she only had on a pair of leggings and a pink T-shirt, her body was nice, and she had the face to match it.

Keyshore wondered what his Eastside nigga LX's old ass was doing to keep such a beautiful young woman so loyal to him while in jail. He respected LX like a gangster, because Joy was head over toes for him.

As soon as Joy stepped on the porch, Lil' Mark wasted no time flirting with her. She waved him off, then followed Keyshore into the house to purchase.

When she left back out, Mark informed her she could get what she purchased for free if she let him take her out. Joy laughed, shook her head, then jumped in her truck.

Keyshore sat back in his seat on the porch as Lil' Mark continued to talk shit to Joy all the way until she pulled off, blowing her horn.

"She is a bad motherfucka'," Keyshore said to Lil' Mark.

Mark never replied. Instead, he pulled out his phone and began strolling down his Instagram page.

CHAPTER 4

Can't Knock the Hustle

Detective Anderson's phone rang nonstop in the homicide unit. In one week, two women, seven kids, and four men had been murdered. And once again, nobody knew shit *or* went to jail for it.

Things got worse by the day, and the feds stepped right in. Although the feds gave a lot of federal gun charges to the black men from the inner city, nothing seemed to stop the unsolved homicides. Victims who lost loved ones complained daily.

Detective Anderson spoke on 19 Action News.

"This 'stop snitching' movement is bullshit. We need people, police, and the community to all come together."

After Detective Anderson finished his speech about violence, he began to speak about the Covid-19 situation and how they were fighting to open schools back up and find a cure. He then put his mask back over his face and walked off, leaving the people asking unanswered questions.

Between the black people killing each other and the police killing the blacks, it left no trust in the system.

Detective Anderson didn't like blacks, but reality really started to kick in on him. Lately, he wasn't feeling all the lawless actions and unfairness the blacks received. He realized the way the system treated them was the cause of violence in the inner cities.

And with Covid-19 only getting worse, and the residents being so unprofessional, the world was headed for self-destruction.

***

Keyshore turned on east Crosier Street, then pulled into the Summit County Jail parking lot. He got out of his rental car with his mask on, because it was required to be worn.

Upon entering the jail, he put a hundred dollars each on Joe, Tino, Snap, and his home girl Nee Nee's books.

On his way out the door again, he locked eyes with a beautiful woman in a sheriff's uniform. The tag on her shirt read 'Officer Brooks.'

He spoke to her briefly, and to his surprise, she

spoke back with a lot of intimacy in her eyes. Keyshore was quick on his game, and his words flowed smooth as he conversated with Deputy Brooks.

With a smile on her face, Miss Brooks told Keyshore the time she went on her lunch break and what she wanted to eat. He reassured her he would be back five minutes before her lunch break.

As he walked back to his car, a few inmates banged on their window that must have known him. He gave a peace sign, then pulled off.

Keyshore couldn't get Miss Brooks off his mind; he couldn't wait until it was time for him to bring her lunch. She was one woman he vowed he would get to know. Although she was a sheriff, Keyshore was smart enough to keep his business private—plus, he had a lot of legit shit going for him anyways, too.

***

Lil' Mark's flight to North Dakota was scheduled to leave in thirty minutes. He grabbed his luggage out of his baby mama Tammy's truck, kissed his daughter, then headed towards the runway.

When he got to the gate, he handed his ticket over, then went through the security checkpoint.

Once he boarded the plane, a beautiful porter ushered him to his seat. Mark grabbed a magazine from the porter, then sat back to relax.

After he landed in North Dakota, the first thing he wanted to do was go ice-fishing. It had been a while since he visited Devil's Lake or hunted wild turkey... Bismarck has always been his fuck-off spot.

The smell of fresh-cooked perch filled the air when he entered his cousin Marshall's restaurant. Marshall greeted Lil' Mark with a hug and informed him how dry business had been since Covid-19 hit. He prayed Lil' Mark had brought some grams of pure Fentanyl, and to his delight, his prayers were answered.

After Lil' Mark ate a plate of fried perch and a bowl of cheese grits with fried green tomatoes on the side, he and Marshall drank a few shots of moonshine, then left the restaurant.

They headed to an apartment Lil' Mark rented by the lake. Mark only brought five grams, but once he did his mix, the grams turned into five thousand grams.

In North Dakota, grams sold for two hundred a gram to the dealers already-cut, and four hundred to the users. The flip was tremendous—Lil' Mark made two-hundred thousand off each gram of uncut. He always split the profit in half with Marshall, so off the five grams that went to five thousand grams, he made half a ticket.

He always gave Marshall a thousand grams at a time after he mixed—mainly for safety purposes—because the shit sold so fast, and Marshall moved so recklessly. But he had to give it to his older cousin; the nigga was a natural hustler.

Marshall boasted loudly and happily when Lil' Mark handed him twenty sandwich bags that contained fifty grams each. He told Mark not to go anywhere because he would be right back in ten minutes.

Marshall knew he would pocket two-hundred thousand off the thousand grams, because he only had to give Mark a hundred thousand.

As promised, Marshall came right back. He ran through four thousand grams in one day. The next day, he purchased the last thousand grams out his own pocket.

Making the money was never the problem for Lil' Mark; getting the money back to *Ohio* was the challenge—he still had over three-hundred thousand from the last time he came stuck in North Dakota...

CHAPTER 5

You Never Know Until You Try

Keyshore pulled back up to the county jail with food he got from his home boy S.Q's restaurant, called "The Gray Area," in Cleveland, Ohio.

Five minutes later, Miss Brooks came out to retrieve her food.

He brought her stuffed lobster tails, fried shrimp with rice, and a bottle of water. She had never had food from the restaurant Keyshore selected before, and he amazed her with how wonderful the food was.

They sat and talked in his car while she ate up, until her lunch break was over. When it was over, she gave Keyshore her cellphone number and promised to let him take her out one day when she was off.

As Miss Brooks walked back into the building for work, she couldn't believe how Keyshore had gained her full attention. Now, she was eager to know more about him, and she prayed he wasn't really in the streets like he told her.

***

After Keyshore left Miss Brooks' job, he decided to check on a building on Brown Street.

The man that had the building for sale was sitting in a car as Keyshore pulled up. He got out—still on the phone—dressed in a suit and signaled for Keyshore to follow him. They toured through the building and talked a little about a few office spaces and prices.

The building was perfect for what Keyshore had in mind for his plan, but he needed a lower price for it, and the standoff he had with the man kept ending with the same price.

When Lil' Mark's number popped up on Keyshore's phone, he excused himself to answer.

Mark updated him on how he was still in North Dakota, and how he still had problems laundering the money or getting it back. Keyshore, being sharp as he was and a quick-thinker, told Lil' Mark that he called at a perfect time.

His plan was to launder the money by buying the building he was at—plus a few more that the man had for sale.

The businessman was all for the plan when Keyshore brought it to his attention. In fact, he had a person Keyshore could drop the money to in North Dakota.

Lil' Mark met with the man that same day and sent the paperwork. He and Keyshore became co-owners of the two buildings and a storefront.

***

Lil' Mark landed in the Akron/Canton airport the next day at about 9:45 in the morning. But as soon as he got off the plane, the feds swarmed him and searched him and his luggage.

Mark couldn't believe it. He felt so disrespected. He promised to make sure his lawyer got word about this, and the plain-clothes officers were pissed when they recovered nothing. The tip they had received promised them that they would recover a large amount of cash, and maybe even some drugs.

Mark cursed loudly as the officers apologized, stating it was simply a case of mistaken identity.

***

That weekend, Miss Brooks called and set a date with Keyshore. They met downtown at the "UP.T.own Lounge." It was early, so the young, wild homies weren't in the building yet. Keyshore promised himself that he would be long gone before it started jumping.

Miss Brooks looked so stunning in her regular clothes, even though she only wore a pair of rock jeans and a lace shirt with red-bottom heels. Just the sight of her smelled of power and attraction.

Her hair in a ponytail—all-natural with no makeup on, either—she stood at only five-foot and two-and-a-half inches with her heels on, but she had the body of a goddess and an ass *so* fat… her 'brown sugar' complexion complimented every aspect of her beauty.

***

She couldn't stop laughing and was all smiles as Keyshore joked and talked shit. After about three shots and a few dances, they decided it was time to cut out and grab a bite to eat.

Miss Brooks followed Keyshore to a small restaurant on the North side, and when they entered, it was breathtaking.

Keyshore had the whole place candlelit, with rose petals sprinkled all over the floor in a path leading to their table. At their table, a bottle of very expensive red wine sat next to two wine glasses and some more candles.

He pulled Miss Brooks' chair out for her to sit

in as slow-jam music played, and the chef himself appeared as if on-cue with their food in-hand.

Miss Brooks was damn-near in tears; this was the most romantic experience she had felt in years. Keyshore's charm was strong, and she couldn't thank him enough.

They ate, laughed, sipped wine, and sang to the old-school slow jams together.

After they left the restaurant, Keyshore walked Miss Brooks to her car, gave her a hug, opened her door for her, and closed it behind her.

When she got in, Miss Brooks let her window down after she started her car and thanked Keyshore both for showing her such a great night and being such a gentleman.

***

Miss Brooks drove home, deep in her thoughts. She wanted to kiss and feel Keyshore hold her *so* bad... He turned her on in ways she hadn't experienced in years. She still couldn't believe he never tried to come onto her or just ask for sex like most men, but for some reason, the demeanor still spelled straight streets to her.

Although he said he wasn't, she knew his kind...

All she could do was pray and continue to take her time with him.

***

When Lil' Mark made it home to his condo downtown, he sent his lawyer a text about the situation from the airport. Ten minutes later, his lawyer was calling, and after they went over all the details, his lawyer promised him answers—and a lawsuit.

***

Mark jumped in the shower, and when he got out, he got dressed and headed straight back out the door.

Keyshore was calling as he pulled out of the parking deck. They talked for about fifteen minutes and agreed to meet at 'the spot' in Kenmore the next day; right now, Mark was on a pussy mission, and he wasn't missing this five-some date he had set up for the night for *anything.*

He met the four ladies at the same white bar he had first met them at. The bar was all the way out on Main Street, so he didn't need to carry a gun—Niggas didn't hang out much at these types of bars.

The night went smooth. They drank and smoked blunts outside, and the women kissed and touched on each other as music played through the night.

"Two mixed women and two white women..." Mark thought to himself as he watched them laugh, touch each other, and dance on the dance floor.

Tonight, was his night, and he popped a few "X" pills just to make sure he fucked like a porno-star when it was on.

When the bar closed, the four girls followed Lil' Mark outside to the parking lot. He walked with two of the women hand-in-hand.

Once they got to their cars, two of the women got in one car, one got in another car, and one jumped in with Mark.

It was 2:30 in the morning as they headed to the hotel, and as soon as they entered the room, it was on. The "X" pills had Mark's dick so hard the whole trip to the hotel, the woman in the car sucked his dick, but he couldn't nut—he knew he would last and make this a moment to remember.

So, they sucked and fucked each other all morning until everyone passed out.

When Lil' Mark finally woke up, he couldn't help but grin. He laid in the middle of the king-sized bed with two women each on both sides of him.

CHAPTER 6

Welcome Home, Rod

Keyshore pulled up on Lane Street, over to his young nigga Rod's mother's house. The whole street was full of cars and people everywhere, because Rod was fresh out from doing eight years in prison. The love was in the air.

Rod had left at the age of eighteen, and now he was twenty-six years old, but he stayed solid, and the respect was always priceless if or when a nigga did that. When the raid-team had kicked in Rod's spot and found a half-brick of heroin, he gave no statement. Instead, he copped out to ten years, and Keyshore paid big money to get him out two years early.

Mark pulled up seconds after Keyshore, parking right behind him. Foreign cars were parked everywhere, but little did Rod know, Mark had a Porsche truck parked up the street for him.

Rod may have been the youngest in the crew, but he also was the best hustler, too.

Word had gotten back about who set Rod up, but Keyshore never spoke about it or let it be known. While Rod was doing his time, Keyshore had sent one of his loyal bitches to visit. She gave Rod the paperwork and had told him that Keyshore wanted to save the murder job for him when he returned.

Rod agreed, and through his whole eight years, he worked out and patiently waited for this day to come.

When Keyshore and Lil' Mark came in the house, Rod went crazy.

He was so happy to see his two close friends—and too much alcohol didn't help. He hugged them both tight and thanked them for taking care of him and his family while he was away.

Keyshore dug into his pocket and gave Rod every bit of ten-thousand dollars—all in hundred-dollar bills. He then told Rod to make sure he called him tomorrow, as he had more for him.

Lil' Mark tossed him some keys and told him, "Keep pressing the unlock buttons until you figure out which vehicle belongs to you."

Everyone ate, drank, and laughed with Rod until he decided it was time for him to cut out and go get some pussy.

The beautiful Mexican woman Rod had with him was the sister of a new friend he'd met in prison. Everyone watched as Rod and his Mexican woman figured out which vehicle Mark brought for him. When Rod figured it out, he jumped in the passenger seat and allowed his girl to drive for him, because he was drunk off his ass.

As Rod pulled off, Keyshore and Lil' Mark shouted, "Welcome home, Rod!"

The night was still young, so Keyshore and Mark headed up to the trap in Kenmore to mix some grams and bag pounds of ice.

***

Rod was up early the next morning, and he left his girl sleeping at the hotel. It had been eight years that he waited to kill Nate.

He still couldn't believe that Nate set him up, and when he got locked up, ran off with two-hundred and fifty-thousand dollars. When Keyshore's lawyer had sent the paperwork, Rods heart was crushed at first, but then it filled with anger.

"Today," Rod promised himself, *"Will be Nate's last day."*

Nate had called Rod's mother a week before Rod got out and left his cell number. He had no reason to think that Rod knew he was the reason he went to jail, and that the police weren't the ones who found his stash.

When Rod pulled up to the address Nate gave him, he had to admit; the four-bedroom house was beautiful. Nate was in the doorway, waiting when Rod got out of his truck.

He invited Rod in and introduced him to his children's mother and his two young sons. Nate's woman cooked breakfast, and they all ate and talked about what Rod's plans for the future were.

As bad as Rod wanted to kill Nate, he knew today wouldn't be the day.

Nate ended up giving Rod five-thousand dollars in cash and a Rolex bust-down watch, telling Rod that whenever he was ready to get back in the game, he had a nice starter for him.

Rod had to smile and really work to hide his anger. He wanted to shoot Nate in the face right in front of his family *so* bad, but out of the respect for the kids, he couldn't.

***

Detective Anderson sat in an all-white, unmarked car a few houses back from Nate's. Nate informed him that Rod would be stopping by, and for safety purposes, numerous of officers and detectives were assigned to stake out.

When Rod jumped in his truck, he noticed a lot of suspicious activity on the street, but Rod remained calm. He backed out of the driveway and drove off as normal.

Just as he thought, when he got to the stop sign, he noticed an unmarked car pulling off from up the street. Nate had eyes on him from the cops and killing him was going to be harder than he thought.

He got on the highway and headed to Cleveland to do some shopping—Rod figured it was best to ease his mind. His anger was getting beyond a boiling point. Nate was a rat and a snake all in one. Being that kind truly made him the dangerous type, and a game-cheater!

Rod knew he and Keyshore had to really sit down at the round table and come up with a great plan for this situation.

CHAPTER 7

The Cheste Boyz

Goldie, Roscoe-Cee, Rusty, and Skelton all stood in front of the corner store on Manchester Road and Thornton Street, selling grams of Fentanyl. Business was booming ever since Keyshore lowered the prices and the potency went up.

Lil' Mark also flooded the 'hood with some truly fire "ice"—the niggas from Ramon Street and V. Odom Boulevard mostly sold that, so the whole valley was jumping; it had been a while since they had the rock.

After Big Choose died and the feds snatched Chez, the niggas from on top of the hill were who you had to shop with… But not anymore.

Rusty hollered for Roscoe-Cee to come to the phone—he had Brain on the phone, from the feds.

A lot of people were happy that Brain was away;

he may have looked harmless, but his name and actions spoke volumes.

Brain was Keyshore's little brother from a different mother and father. Although they weren't blood, there was no limit to what they would do for each other.

The sad part about everything was that they had never been on the streets together since Brain was a kid; every time one came home, the other was going to jail.

Roscoe talked in code to Brain, letting him know everything going on. Brain was glad the young boyz of his that he had hooked Keyshore up with were finally eating good. Although Keyshore hadn't used them for their murder game yet, he made sure he put bands in their pockets.

He wasn't tripping—Brain put the stamp on those young boyz, so it wasn't shit to question or second-guess him.

After Roscoe-Cee hung up with Brain, he gave Rusty his phone back, jumped in his baby mama's car, then pulled off to go meet one of his customers.

Skelton noticed a white Camaro circling the block for the third time in twenty minutes. He clutched his waist for his gun, and Rusty and Goldie followed suit off instinct.

The white Camaro turned off Thornton Street

back onto Manchester Road towards them.

In broad daylight, like a movie, the windows came down and guns appeared, firing shots.

Rusty was hit in the arm before he could draw his gun, but Skelton was a natural; he let off thirty shots from his .40 with an extended clip. Goldie had a .357 revolver, and he also fired six shots back of his own.

The Camaro crashed up against the sidewalk about a block up from the store.

Skelton slapped another clip in his gun, then raced down towards the crashed car. Goldie followed as he loaded six more bullets in his own gun.

As they approached the car, they could see the brains of the driver's head against the windshield—he was dead for sure. The passenger was holding his neck and blood S.Q.uirted through his fingers. He looked to be hit in the chest and arms. In the back, a young kid that couldn't be any older than fifteen years old laid slumped, eyes open and gun still in his hand with a bullet hole in the head.

Goldie shot the passenger two more times in the head, then he and Skelton fled towards Blanch Street.

When Roscoe-Cee pulled back up to the corner store, police cars and ambulances were everywhere. His heart was racing—he had only been gone for ten minutes; he couldn't understand what could have happened that quick. Before he could get out of his car, Ronda from the store was at his door.

Ronda told him, "Rusty was shot and his whole arm was hanging off—he was rushed to the hospital. Down the street, the three people that shot Rusty crashed, and it looks like they been shot to death."

Roscoe-Cee couldn't believe the news he got. When he asked where Skelton and Goldie were at, Ronda went silent.

She took a deep breath, then told Roscoe the police got security footage with them shooting at the car, and the car shooting at them. As far as she knew, they were somewhere hiding out, and had better be considering getting out of town.

Roscoe-Cee punched the steering wheel of his baby mama's car and cursed loudly.

"Things were going so good—how could something like this just happen out the clear blue?!"

***

Detective Anderson received the call about three men being killed, and one man being shot in the arm and rushed to the hospital. He raced to the scene on Manchester Road, where yellow tape sectioned off the crime scene.

The victims, dead on the scene, were still left in the white Camaro. Detective Anderson shook his head at the fiasco.

Police officers working the scene informed him that some security footage of the crime was recovered, and two suspects needed to be identified—most likely, the suspects were the killers.

Just hearing that news brought a smile to Detective Anderson's face. His luck with all these killings had been terrible until now.

After they lifted the car with the dead bodies onto the flat bed and hauled them off to the crime lab, Detective Anderson got into his unmarked car and raced back to headquarters.

As soon as he reviewed the tapes, he knew exactly who the two shooters involved were. He smacked hands with the lady detective, Gina, and they quickly put murder warrants out for Chris Gibson—A.K.A. 'Goldie'—and Sam Johnson, A.K.A. 'Skelton.'

***

Rusty laid in the hospital, heavily drugged and fresh out of surgery. The doctors couldn't save his right arm—they had to cut it off from the elbow down.

Although he wasn't charged for the murders, the police wanted answers. They knew that he knew the two guys that killed the three dudes in the Camaro.

The video didn't show Rusty with any guns, so they couldn't charge him or link him to the crime itself, but they could place him at the scene and show he knew the shooters.

CHAPTER 8

Murder Bout Money

Nate was practically on fire with rage when news got back to him about his young shooters being killed on Manchester Road.

He sent the hit because he wanted to fuck up Keyshore's business. The fact Keyshore that had Goldie, Roscoe-Cee, Rusty, and Skelton buying from him now put a bad taste in Nate mouth. Not to mention, they chalked him and never gave him the money for the last pack he fronted them.

Nate paced back and forth at his trap spot on East Avenue as he spoke on the phone with his gossiping-ass cousin, Sue.

Sue always knew all the 'hood news in the Valley. If you ever needed the scoop, she was the go-to.

But Nate was nervous, too—he prayed word didn't get to Detective Anderson that the dudes that got killed were sent by him. Nate was truly a threat; he was about murder, plus he was a snitch with a lot of money.

Now that his homeboy Rod was home, Nate really prayed that he would jump back in the game and fuck with him. He knew the power of Rod's hustle, and he needed him back on his team.

The only reason Nate had told on him was because he felt like Rod was gonna cut him off since he was starting to get big money.

Jealousy made him cross a loyal friend, and deep down inside, guilt was burning him up. He knew it was wrong to set Rod up, and he knew he only faced eighteen months with the case he caught...

But yet and still, he dropped a dime on Rod and stole his stash.

***

After Nate hung up with Sue, he left the trap on foot. He never parked his truck around the trap—the last thing he wanted was Detective Anderson fucking with him.

It seemed like after he set Rod up, the police never stopped sending him on missions. The shit was really starting to wear on him, and he was sick of being Detective Anderson's little snitch.

Nate really wanted his full street life back, but he knew it would never happen.

Once he got on Moon Street, he jumped in his Ford F-150 and hauled ass from the West side.

Nate had started really enjoying Barberton—nobody out there was hip to him, and he had it on lock.

But he also knew that he needed to get Keyshore and Lil' Mark out of the way in the 'hood.

He quickly texted Detective Anderson and set up a meeting date.

***

Keyshore couldn't believe what he was hearing when Rod called him with the news about Goldie and Skelton. He needed to talk to Roscoe-Cee really bad, and he had a bad feeling the police might snatch Rusty from the hospital.

Rod also updated him about Nate and the police situation. Killing Nate wasn't going to be a cake-walk, and he knew that, but Keyshore was a great listener, and both sucked up all the info and made mental notes, as well.

For some reason, the situation spelled 'Nate' all over it to him, and he wasn't going to rest until he figured it out.

***

Miss Brooks and Keyshore talked on the phone a lot and went on several dates as time went on.

She couldn't seem to find anything bad out about Keyshore, aside from having been to jail and federal prison for selling drugs and having a gun, but that was years ago.

She realized it was time to let her guard down and really give things a chance. Miss Brooks loved how confident Keyshore was, and how he was always a gentleman to her.

Tonight, she had a surprise for him.

She smiled to herself as she sent him a text. When Keyshore texted back that he could be free for her anytime, she smiled even wider. She then set a date and informed him that everything would be her treat.

***

Roscoe-Cee followed Nate two cars behind as Nate headed to the apartment that he'd stashed drugs at in Barberton.

Roscoe-Cee couldn't believe his luck—when he rode down Moon Street, he had caught Nate getting into his truck. The money on Nate's head was worth a lot right now, seeing as Goldie and Skelton were on the run, and the work Keyshore fronted got found by the police.

When Nate pulled into a small lot where the cars from the apartments used for parking, Roscoe-Cee pulled right next to him.

Careful as Nate usually was, today he was slipping and was caught off-guard as he argued with his baby's mother about where he was last night.

Nate got out his truck, still fussing with his baby mama on the phone. Roscoe-Cee jumped out his car, gun in hand in broad daylight.

By the time Nate looked up to realize someone was walking up on him, it was too late.

Nate dropped his cellphone and reached for his gun in his belt around his waist, but it was pointless—Roscoe-Cee had the ups, and he wasn't playing.

Bullets fired nine times from Roscoe-Cee's 40 Cal', striking Nate in the face, chest, legs, and arms. Nate was dead as soon as he hit the ground, but Roscoe-Cee still walked up on his lifeless body and put two more bullets in his head for good measure.

He could still hear Nate's baby mama screaming Nate's name through the phone as he ran back to his car and sped off.

She hung up her phone when Nate didn't respond after several times of wailing his name, and quickly called Detective Anderson to tell him she heard several gun shots when she and Nate were on the phone.

"Something is wrong!" she shouted to Detective Anderson, "Nate's somewhere, shot—I can feel it!"

Detective Anderson told her to calm down, then asked if she knew where he was going. She had no clue, but before Detective Anderson could hang up, his radio went off, speaking, "Shots fired—one man down with multiple gunshot wounds."

Sure enough, when Detective Anderson made it to the crime scene in Barberton, it was Nate, laid out and dead.

His heart dropped, and he had to fight away the tears. No one never knew the true secret about his relationship with Nate—Detective Anderson was Nate's biological father.

He had never shared the facts with Nate because he and Nate's mother agreed it wasn't a great ideal. Detective Anderson was a married man, so he and Nate's mother vowed to keep the child a secret.

But as his son laid there, motionless, with lifeless eyes wide open, hurt turned to anger, and you could see the rage in Detective Anderson face.

Detective Anderson pulled out his cellphone and dialed Nate's mothers number. She answered on the third ring, but dropped the phone in tears when he gave her the news about their son.

Detective Anderson couldn't hold himself back any longer—hearing his son's mother's wailing cry broke him down in tears. He quickly got into his tinted, unmarked car and locked the doors.

He couldn't stop the tears; they came down harder than he had ever cried as he listened to his son's mother bawling.

***

Roscoe-Cee texted Keyshore and told him, "Nate is no longer with the world of life anymore. The game he dishonored finally caught up with him."

As soon as Keyshore received the text from Roscoe-Cee, he called him. Roscoe-Cee picked up on the first ring.

Keyshore was proud that the job got taken care of quick, but he was also very concerned about the situation with Goldie, Rusty, and Skelton, so he told Roscoe-Cee to meet him in Kenmore at the trap.

When Keyshore pulled up to the trap, Lil' Mark and Roscoe-Cee were sitting on the porch, smoking a blunt. He dapped them both, then sat on the porch banister.

Rod pulled up fifteen minutes later on a motorcycle with the biggest smile in the world. Just hearing the news about Nate's police-kissing ass was music to his ears.

Keyshore decided it was best to chill out of Akron and start trapping somewhere out of town, but he wanted to make sure they got Goldie and Skelton out the city safe, first.

Lil' Mark let him know that he already had them enroute to North Dakota as they spoke, and so far, everything was going smooth with the ride.

Rod, however, being on parole, knew it wouldn't be safe for him to leave, and Keyshore agreed with him.

As for Roscoe-Cee, he figured he would duck off in W.V. and get money all through the cities there.

With Rusty still being in the hospital, everyone was on pins and needles. He played a big part of the team, and they needed him to remain solid.

Keyshore had sent his lawyer to talk with Rusty, and as far as he knew, Rusty was cool and remaining solid.

So, the wait was just the wait, and everyone continued doing them.

Roscoe-Cee left to W.V., and Goldie and Skelton made it safe to North Dakota that same night.

CHAPTER 9

Crips Invade the East Side

With Young Ruler having so much love in the East side, it felt impossible for Joy to catch up with him. Plus, the fact that they both were Bloods left everyone that Joy needed help from in a neutral position.

LX sent word to Joy not to worry about it; he would take care of shit with Ruler whenever their time came.

Joy's pride was in the way, though, and she couldn't acceP.T. the disrespect.

Lil' Mark was Joy's best help. She knew he wanted to fuck her bad, and if that's what it took to get Young Ruler, *"So be it,"* she thought.

Joy called Lil' Mark and agreed to let him take her out—as long as it was not in Akron.

Later on that night, they met up with each other in Mansfield, Ohio at a small bar downtown.

When Joy entered the bar an hour after Lil' Mark had been there, his jaw dropped. Joy looked beautiful in her tight Gucci jeans with matching shirt, and Gucci red-bottom heels with a matching bag to top it off.

All eyes were on her as she swaggered over toward Lil' Mark at the bar.

Lil' Mark—who was already tipsy—shouted for the bartender to get Joy whatever she was drinking.

Joy had to admit; Lil' Mark was looking very handsome as his jewels glistened in the light.

She ordered a tropical drink that seemed very strong with a little too much vodka as Mark gave her a friendly hug, and they headed off to a private table that sat in the back of the bar.

Lil' Mark's charm was on, and he kept Joy laughing and tapping him. He was shocked at how he and Joy seemed to be getting along so well. Fine as Joy was, he knew this young lady was a stone-cold killer, and it was just so hard to believe.

When Jay-Z's song, "*Somehow Someway*" came on, Joy got up and started dancing in front of Mark, singing along with the song. She was on her third drink and feeling *very* good.

Lil' Mark bobbed his head back and forth as he watched Joy sing and dance. He knew Joy's loyalty was with LX, but he didn't care—LX wasn't his dude. Lil' Mark only met LX once through Keyshore, and Keyshore was the one close to LX.

Joy had so much fun with Mark, and before they knew it, the light came on and a waiter yelled, "Last call for alcohol!"

Mark asked if she wanted another drink to go, but he knew she was already drunk.

Joy drank the rest of the drink in front of her and shouted, "Fuck it, why not? Get me one to go!"

When they got outside to the parking lot, Mark told Joy he thought it would be best if she rode with him and that he would have his homeboy drive her car to Akron in the morning.

Joy kissed him right on the mouth, then whispered in his ear, "Mark, I want you to fuck me *real* good..."

Lil' Mark laughed. Joy was drunk, and although he really wanted the pussy, he didn't want it under these circumstances. He opened the door to his truck and put Joy inside, then headed home to Akron.

By the time they reached Akron, Joy was knocked out, and she refused to wake up or even tell Lil' Mark where to drop her off at. Lil' Mark had no choice; he took her to his apartment downtown.

After he parked in the parking garage, he tapped Joy, who surprisingly woke up and was willing to come inside to his place. When they entered his apartment, Joy was impressed how nice and neat Mark's place was. Lil' Mark was a gentleman, to her surprise—he offered her his room and said he would take the couch.

Joy took a shower and put on one of Lil' Mark's t-shirts, then quickly passed out on his bed.

In the meantime, Lil' Mark laid on his couch watching *Sports Center* until he dozed off.

When he woke the next morning, Joy was up cooking breakfast. The smell of bacon and eggs filled the apartment, so Lil' Mark got up and went in the kitchen.

The sight of Joy in his shirt with no panties cooking breakfast had his dick hard.

When Joy finally looked back because she felt Mark watching, she smiled.

He walked up behind her and hugged her from the back, whispering, "Aren't I a lucky man, to have you cooking breakfast, baby...?"

Joy swatted him away and laughed, then thanked Lil' Mark for being such a gentleman the previous night. She told him she liked him, but they had to keep it a secret.

That morning, Joy and Lil' Mark made passionate love after they ate breakfast. They fucked in the kitchen, the bed, the living room, *and* the shower. After what seemed like hours of lovemaking, they laid in bed holding each other.

Joy told Lil' Mark how Young Ruler chalked her and refuse to pay her. She told him that that was how it had been for months, and she still hadn't caught up with him, mainly because they both were Bloods and nobody, she fucked with would get involved. And yet, Young Ruler had all the young Bloods riding for him and hustling for him.

Just for her, Lil' Mark put the call in for twenty-thousand on Young Ruler, and just like that, the Crips got involved.

***

Young Ruler pulled into ABS cellphone shop on Arlington to pay his phone bill. He never noticed the black and yellow van that trailed him ever since he passed Six Corners after leaving from his aunt's house in Eastland Woods.

Blue Rag, Rolen, Lil' Cuz, and T.Q. parked across the street from the phone store, then quickly jumped out and ran across Arlington to ABS.

They stood close to the sidewalk like they were waiting on the bus as they waited for Young Ruler to come back out.

Soon, Young Ruler came back out, and he jumped in his car, heading towards where the Crips all stood.

The moment he stopped to wait for the ongoing traffic to clear so he could go up Arlington, Blue Rag and T.Q. ran up and started shooting into his car.

He never saw it coming.

As bullets showered his body, Rolen and Lil' Cuz also emptied their clips into his car. They then ran across Arlington where their van was parked in the cut and pulled out.

Young Ruler's car crashed into a pole and was hit by another car, but he was well dead before his car even moved into traffic.

It was another cold-hearted killing in broad daylight, and nobody claimed to witness shit.

Detective Anderson pulled up to a scene that was filled with police cars and ambulances everywhere.

***

When the news came through that Young Ruler got killed, the Bloods on the East side were pissed off.

But Joy couldn't believe how fast Lil' Mark put the murder play down for her. She told him the situation that morning, and by four p.m., Young Ruler was dead—that was big to her.

Lil' Mark really earned some great respect in her heart with that statement.

Joy might have loved the move Lil' Mark put down for her, but what she didn't realize was that that move was the start of a gang war.

Word got back to the young Bloods that some Crips killed Young Ruler, and that same night, Lil' Cuz got killed on Wildwood Avenue, and Rolen got shot five times but survived.

The Crips struck right back that next morning. Two Bloods got killed on Baird Hill, and four others got shot but lived.

***

The beef went on for weeks, and now it had come back that Joy paid the Crips to kill Young Ruler. She was in violation, so the Bloods burnt down two houses she owned on the East side and kidnapped her main man, Zeek.

When Joy got the call that they had Zeek, her heart dropped. They wanted her life, or a hundred-thousand dollars for Zeek back.

As soon as she hung up from the ransom call, LX was calling her cellphone. Before she could get a word out, he was screaming and disrespecting her.

Joy didn't realize how much she fucked up until now, but she still felt she wasn't in the wrong. However, it was too late to tuck her tail, so she screamed back at LX and told him she wasn't going to be one of his bitches anymore, then disconnected from his call.

CHAPTER 10

Murder About Money

Detective Anderson questioned Rusty for the fifth time in a week, yet Rusty continued to give him the same story every time.

He knew Rusty would be released from the hospital today, and he was pissed he couldn't charge or connect him in the murder on Manchester Road.

Rusty gave Detective Anderson none of his attention as he went on with the same questions he asked every day, it seemed.

Finally, Rusty spoke up; he told the detective he'd had enough. Not only was he mentally drained, but he was also still dealing with the fact that he had lost an arm.

Detective Anderson decided to give up and acceP.T. he lost this battle. He gave Rusty his card and told him to give him a call if any new information popped into his head or if he found out anything that would help.

When he finally left with the two APD officers that were assisting him, Rusty called his girl to come pick him up.

***

Miss Brooks and Keyshore met up at a small, French onion soup shop in Canton, Ohio.

When Keyshore pulled into the parking lot, she was already waiting on him. Miss Brooks got out her car and waved Keyshore to do the same.

Keyshore couldn't help but smile; she looked so beautiful and excited. When he reached where she was at the door, he hugged her and kissed her gently on the lips. He then opened the door for her, and they both entered the soup shop.

Miss Brooks' order consisted of a slow-cooked chicken and vegetable soup, and some crusty bread with Swiss cheese on the side, and a glass of red wine. Keyshore ordered an American-style tomato soup with croutons, a buttered grilled cheese toast sandwich, and a glass of sweet tea.

This was quite a different style of dinner for Keyshore, and he was truly liking the creativity from Miss Brooks.

They ate and talked about all kinds of different things—Miss Brooks was shocked at how

Keyshore was so much of an entrepreneur. He had great plans and goals, and he knew how he wanted to achieve them.

When the bill came, Keyshore reached in his pocket for the credit card in his wallet. Miss Brooks smacked his hand and told him she was paying for everything tonight.

Keyshore couldn't help but laugh before he apologized and told her he had forgotten.

After they left the soup shop, they went to the Hall of Fame Museum.

Keyshore was surprised at how much Miss Brooks knew about people that played football. They held hands as they viewed different exhibits. It shocked Keyshore when Miss Brooks told him the Cleveland Browns was her team—he kissed her on the cheek and said they were his team, too.

By the time they left, it was dark.

Miss Brooks had Keyshore follow her to a hotel room she already had reserved.

After she parked, she jumped in the car with Keyshore and told him that this was where the night ended with them.

Keyshore smiled, and was about to turn his car off, but Miss Brooks stopped him.

"We are going to the bar to have some drinks first," she informed Keyshore.

Keyshore followed her directions until they

pulled up to a sports bar in North Canton.

They played pool, shot darts, and got a good buzz. The sports bar was really laid back—Keyshore enjoyed the mixed crowd. He couldn't believe how cool the white people were—he had never been around white people like he was tonight. These people weren't people he was doing business with, or police that hated blacks; they were cool, fun, and respectful, but most of all, they treated him like a normal human.

By the time Keyshore and Miss Brooks made it back to the hotel room, it was 2:30 a.m.

As soon as the door shut, Miss Brooks got naked and headed to the shower. Keyshore had to admire her beautiful body, and he couldn't help himself—his dick got hard just at the sight of her naked body.

Keyshore quickly tore off his own clothes, then joined her in the shower. They washed each other up, gently kissed, and held each other.

Tonight was *the* night, and Miss Brooks wanted it to be right.

After they got out the shower, Miss Brooks rubbed Keyshore down with baby oil. Then he returned the favor, and after that, he slowly kissed her on the lips.

Miss Brooks made Keyshore promise that he wouldn't hurt her if she gave her heart and body to him, and he gladly agreed.

They made love the whole morning and all the way up into the afternoon.

Keyshore laid in bed, watching Miss Brooks sleep in his arms. She was all the woman he could have ever wanted, and he was so glad that they had taken this step forward.

He knew it was nearing time for him to get out the streets. By the grace of God, he hadn't been to jail in years and not only was he still alive, but well off, too.

His mind wandered and raced—there was so much going on in his life. He even thought about how he killed his first cousin, and how the evil of money had turned his cousin against him.

The game was the game, and he couldn't name many who made it out alive without doing life in the feds.

This was his call, and it was time to walk away and make a family and live righteously.

***

Rusty's girl pulled up thirty minutes after he called, and he looked in both directions before he jumped into the front passenger seat. He kissed her on the cheek as she pulled away from the hospital.

Once they got to the West side, he had her pull

into the Boost Mobile phone store's parking lot on Coply Road and go inside to buy him a flip phone. When she got back in the car and gave him the phone, he quickly dialed Keyshore's number.

After calling three times and getting no answer from Keyshore, Rusty sent a text instead, then called Lil' Mark, who picked up on the second ring. Lil' Mark told Rusty to meet him at the trap in Kenmore in an hour, then disconnected.

When Lil' Mark hung up with Rusty, he looked over at Joy, who really seemed lost in a deep daze.

Ever since the Bloods wanted to kill Joy, Lil' Mark kept her with him, and tomorrow, the one-hundred thousand for Zeek's ransom was scheduled to be paid. Joy only had forty-thousand, but Lil' Mark had covered the rest.

Joy was immensely hurt, but angry at the same time, and that spelled a lot of trouble for the future. She couldn't believe how LX turned on her when she was so loyal to him... she figured the beef was really about the drugs she sold for him.

Lil' Mark reached over and softly rubbed Joy's arm.

When she looked over at him, he told her, "Baby don't stress. Shit going to be cool; you're with me, now."

Joy smiled and thanked him for all the help and love he showed.

But Lil' Mark knew Joy would never go out like this, and the killing had just begun. If only he could get Joy to take a trip with him to North Dakota, maybe he could convince her to start a new life there with him...

***

Lil' Mark and Joy were sitting in the car when Rusty and his girl pulled up on the trap in Kenmore.

Lil' Mark jumped out, and when Rusty got out of the car with only one arm, it broke his heart to see, but he was glad Rusty made it, and more importantly, that he didn't snitch.

He had plans to send Rusty down to West Virginia with Roscoe-Cee, or to North Dakota with Goldie and Skelton. The choice was Rusty's, and that was the main reason he had him meet him at the trap.

After they talked and laughed for about an hour, Rod pulled up, and Keyshore texted back that he was ducked off somewhere and he would meet with him tomorrow.

Rod hugged Rusty, then gave him a few bands to put in his pocket.

Rusty decided he wanted to go to North Dakota instead of West Virginia, and Lil' Mark was very pleased with his decision.

After they finished smoking the blunt, Rod rolled up, everyone went their separate ways, and as each car pulled off, Detective Anderson—who was parked down the street in an unmarked car—wrote down each license plate.

***

Keyshore and Miss Brooks enjoyed each other all weekend. They made love and hung out, too.

Once they checked out of the hotel room, Keyshore walked her to her car, hugged her, and then kissed her passionately. Love was truly in the air for both, and boy did it feel good to share the feeling.

After Miss Brooks pulled off, Keyshore got in his car and texted Rusty to meet him at the barber shop on V. Odom.

Keyshore pulled up to the barbershop twenty-five minutes later, but Rusty hadn't pulled up yet, so he went in and got a lineup from K. Rock.

As Keyshore and K. Rock talked while he lined up his hair, Rusty came walking in.

Keyshore smiled. He was happy to see Rusty and know he was okay, even though he lost an arm. Rusty sat in the barber's chair across from Keyshore and got his hair cut by Kenny J.

After they finished getting haircuts, they all

went outside to smoke a few blunts.

As always, before long, Keyshore had the barber shop's front yard packed with people. Kenny J. and K. Rock didn't mind—it brought them a lot of extra business every time.

Rusty updated Keyshore on his decision to go to North Dakota to hustle with Goldie and Skelton. Keyshore thought it was a great choice—plus, he knew Lil' Mark's cousin Marshall had shit on smash out there, anyways.

Keyshore gave Rusty a few bands and told him he would catch up with him later; he had a lot of running around to do, and ever since Miss Brooks came into his life, he thought a lot more about making his exit out of the game.

He waited for Rusty to get in the car he was driving before he pulled out.

But as soon as Rusty went to open the door, an all-black Tahoe truck pulled up beside him, and what happened next seemed like it was all in slow motion.

The window came down, and two guys with masks on fired several shots from the back seat and passenger seat.

Rusty never saw it coming.

Keyshore jumped out of his car, gun in hand, and started shooting at the truck. A few of the 'hood homies also fired at the truck, but it sped off and nobody got hit.

When Keyshore got to where Rusty was laid out in front of his car, his heart dropped. Rusty was dead on sight, and he had no idea where the hit had come from.

The sound of sirens coming rang out, and Keyshore knew it was best he left the scene before the cops came. He jumped in his car and headed to Kenmore Boulevard—to the trap.

As he parked, Lil' Mark, Joy, and Rod were pulling up, too.

Keyshore still had Rusty's blood all over his clothes as they all entered the house. Everyone sat in silence for what seemed like an hour before Keyshore spoke up and broke the silence.

"Tonight, somebody dies for this!"

The only problem was that they had no clue who the fuck killed Rusty. The only thing Keyshore could think of was that it had to have come about as revenge for the three dudes Goldie and Skelton had killed on Manchester.

Just then, Lil' Mark got a text that Zeek was let free, and when he showed it to Joy, her heart melted. She prayed that he made it out alive and that they kept their word once the money got paid.

Five minutes after the text came through, Zeek called Joy to let her know he was okay, and she could feel the energy in his voice. Zeek wasn't happy about the situation, and murder was on his mind—Joy already knew he would be ready to ride *hard.*

CHAPTER 11

Covid 19 Everybody on A Curfew and Required Mask On

It was going on a year, and the government still hadn't found a cure for the Covid-19 outbreak.

Ohio was being put on lockdown with a ten o'clock p.m. curfew, and businesses were being shut down left and right. Everywhere you went, you had to have a mask on, or you could be slapped with a fine.

The world was in an uproar, and the U.S President wasn't doing his job well enough for the people. Not only was there Covid-19, but a race war was also blooming due to the ongoing police killings of blacks and the support of white supremacy from the President.

Things became overwhelming for Keyshore. With people driving around the 'hood with masks on, you couldn't tell who was who. The few businesses he had started with Lil' Mark weren't able to do any good with Covid-19 shutting shit down.

Not to mention, Rusty was dead, and he still hadn't got word on that, which meant the truth would come out who knows when, and Brain was set to come home from the Feds in a few more months.

Keyshore's mind was just racing—he was well off, so making sure Brain was cool wasn't a problem, but he wanted to show Brain a different way from the streets. Brain was very smart, and he had his own money still stashed out there, but Keyshore wanted to welcome him home to the legit business world.

But Covid-19 was fucking up everything, Rusty was gone, Goldie and Skelton were on the run for murder, Demond was dead...

"And guess who killed him?" Keyshore thought out loud as he drank Hennessy out of the bottle in his car, parked on Fern Street.

***

The city of Akron, Ohio looked like a ghost town. By eleven p.m., nobody was outside, and the stores were closed—the only thing that seemed to be open were the gas stations.

Little Zeek pulled into the BP on Grant Street, put his red mask over his mouth, then got out to get gas and a box of *Black & Mild.*

Detective Anderson was calling it a night as he left from the South side, leaving off Cole Avenue. When he got to the stop sign of Grant and South, he noticed Little Zeek getting into a car.

He sat at the stop sign until Little Zeek pulled off, heading up South Street towards Brown Street. He followed behind Little Zeek, which made Little Zeek more alert seeing as it was the only other car on the street.

Little Zeek grabbed his gun from off the seat—he wasn't taking any more chances after being kidnapped. The last thing on Little Zeek's mind was the police; he thought it was the same people who snuck up on him at his baby mama's house and forced him into a trunk at gunpoint.

He turned his music up and made himself seem relaxed and unaware.

Detective Anderson didn't realize the situation wasn't a good idea at all, but ever since his son was shot down in the streets, he felt it was his duty to solve that case.

Not calling for backup or calling in that he was following a suspect was the worst mistake he ever made in his life.

Little Zeek turned off Inman Street to Baird Street; it was the perfect place to open fire and not get caught. He parked, and the unmarked car Detective Anderson drove parked behind him.

Zeek waited for a few minutes to see if the people in the tinted-out charger would get out, but no one did.

So, he decided to make the first move, and jumped out with two guns in his hands and started shooting.

Detective Anderson was taken off guard.

Before he could realize Little Zeek had a weapon, bullets him in the neck, shoulder, and hand.

He quickly ducked down, then radioed. “Officer down, shots fired on the corner of Inman and Baird Street!”

Little Zeek walked up on the tinted-out Charger as he continued shooting. When he got up to the driver’s side and noticed a body laying sideways in the front seat and barely moving, he fired five more shots, then jumped back into his car.

He sped off up the street, then whipped his car into the garage where his uncle stayed. Zeek entered the house through the garage.

His uncle was old and sat exactly where Little Zeek knew he would be—in front of the TV, in his chair.

Zeek gave his uncle a hug and asked him if he was hungry. His uncle had Alzheimer’s, so it was like he was back in a childish stage. Zeek usually had his girlfriend take care of him, but a lot of times, he did it himself.

As he prepared his uncle a plate of leftovers from the night before, he heard sirens and could see police lights flashing all the way up the streets from where his uncle lived.

He smiled to himself and said, “I bet nobody *else* will follow Zeek the God.”

Police, homicide, ambulances, and even the Channel 8 News crew flooded the scene of what appeared to be to be an officer down.

Detective Anderson had already been rushed to the city hospital, but sad to say, he died in the ambulance on the way.

You know what they say: a lot comes out about a person when they die.

Detective Anderson’s past was well-guarded from the public thanks to his fellow officers; the only thing they couldn’t cover up was him not following the protocol. Because Detective Anderson never alerted the station or any officers that he was investigating someone or something, it made it extremely hard to determine whether the shooting happened on or off duty.

The next morning, Little Zeek woke up to a thousand text messages about a police officer being killed down the street from his uncle’s house. He was in total shock—he couldn't believe he had killed a cop.

His mind began to race.

"Did anyone witness it? Did the unmarked car have video dash? Who was the cop? What should I do with the car I drove? Should I get rid of the guns?" he thought.

Little Zeek got off the couch and texted Joy to come pick him up over at his uncle's ASAP.

By the time he got out the shower, Joy texted that she was in the driveway. He quickly got dressed, grabbed the two guns he killed the officer with, and headed out the door.

Joy really didn't like being on the East side. Ever since she had Young Ruler killed, the Blood love wasn't the same. She looked side to side every second until Little Zeek came out and jumped into the rental car she was driving.

Little Zeek shut the door and told Joy to jump on the highway; he needed to run to Cleveland. He updated Joy on the whole situation as they drove, and she was shocked, but very happy.

After he tossed the guns into Lake Erie, they pulled to The Grey Area on Euclid to holler at P.T.

As they waited for P.T. to pull up, Joy got a text from Lil' Mark saying, "The officer that got killed last night was Detective Anderson."

She flashed her phone to Zeek so he could read the text.

Zeek shook his head, then said, “At least I got one of them motherfuckers we don’t gotta worry about anymore!”

Joy bust out laughing—she had to agree.

Once P.T. pulled up, they hung out with him for the rest of the day. He was well-respected in Cleveland—Cliffview represented him and S.Q., and the niggas from the valley in Akron had love.

Joy had met P.T. and S.Q. through Keyshore, and her gangsta ways brought a liking to P.T. It wasn’t about sex, though—just good business and real nigga shit.

By the time they left from hanging out with P.T., it was close to ten p.m. Zeek wanted to make sure he got rid of his car, so they had Andy the Handyman pick it up and scrap it for parts. He was texting Zeek, letting him know when he was all done and thanking him for the parts he got for free.

Joy pulled up on Lil’ Mark soon as they got back in Akron, and Zeek made sure he put it on his bucket list to ask Joy what was up with her and Lil’ Mark.

Lil’ Mark was at a new trap spot that he and Joy shared on Manchester Road.

When they pulled up, Joy gave him the “don’t say nothing around Little Zeek” look, and he caught it on cue.

The three of them sat on the porch and smoked a few blunts, talking until Zeek's phone went off and he asked Joy to drop him off to handle some business.

MURDER BOUT MONEY

I stand tall, refusing to ever give up.
Maybe it's the warrior in me,
Maybe it's my pride.
You got me loving you so much,
I can't get over you...
Nefarious as my life has been, you've brought me joy.
I've partitioned all your love into my energy,
Its passion is peculiar and significant.
Welcome to the world of no second chances—
Murder Bout Money,
It's not the game; it's the way we are living....
Whoever said, "loyalty and respect doesn't matter,"
Is probably in the grave for dishonor.
Good business leads to great credit,
Teamwork makes a dream work,
And chickens talk...

CHAPTER 12

A Vacation to Remember

The winter hit hard in Akron, Ohio. It was December 28th, 2020, and Keyshore just hung up with the airport station after booking a flight. He made reservations for him and Miss Brooks vacation to L.A., California.

Their flight was leaving tomorrow, and he wanted to really make things special for Miss Brooks.

He had reservations too a five-star hotel in Hollywood, laid out with rose petals leading to the hot tub, and he had a special dinner that would be served an hour after they checked in.

Keyshore had to smile at himself—he had a great surprise for Miss Brooks, and a lot of gifts to give her.

Snow was everywhere when Keyshore looked out his apartment window.

He quickly got dressed, as he and Rod had

some business to attend to in less than an hour and a half; a lot of tension was boiling in the 'hood again, and as bad as Keyshore wanted everyone to move as one, things were sectioned and clicked off. There was up the way, down the way, the Cheste, the projects, city view...

It just didn't make sense to Keyshore. Growing up, they all stuck together and were just the "Valley Boyz," which later became "V-Not."

Keyshore decided that today was a great day to drive his 2020 F-150 truck because there was so much snow outside.

When he got inside, he took a deep breath of the new truck smell. He was the first driver to ever drive this truck—he had bought it fresh off the showroom floor.

He headed to Rod's house out in Ellet, and it occurred to him that this was his first time going to Rod's house since he had it built from the ground up.

When Keyshore pulled into the driveway, it was breathtaking.

Rod had a four-car garage and a beautiful brick-style house with a huge backyard.

He texted Rod and told him he was outside, and three minutes later, Rod waved him to come in from the side door.

Keyshore entered the house's side door, which led to the finished basement that Rod had his 'man cave' laid out in.

Rod was a chain-smoking type of nigga, so as soon as Keyshore sat down, he was passing him a lit blunt. Then he sat on the bar and started rolling another blunt.

The weed was really good, and that was mostly what the meeting was about. As they smoked blunt after blunt and talked prices, Keyshore had to give it to his little homie Rod; he was a hustling motherfucker.

Rod updated Keyshore on the beef within the 'hood and informed him that there wasn't shit he could do about it. Keyshore was older now, and he realized Rod had a lot of power and control in the 'hood with the youngsters. Brain would be home soon, and he also would control a lot in the 'hood, so Keyshore took Rod's advice and allowed shit to be what it was going to be.

Before he left Rod's house, he went into his truck and gave Rod a Gucci bag full of money for the load of weed that soon would be coming. He then let Rod know that he was taking Miss Brooks on vacation tomorrow, and he would be gone for a week.

He wasn't worried about the weed; he knew Rod would hold his share down or even sell it if a good lick came before he returned.

After Keyshore left Rod's place, he stopped at the Strait-laced smoke shop and grabbed a few weed pipes and a box of blunts.

His main man Los was doing good through the Covid-19 circumstances; he always had the blunts you wanted for cheap, and all the cool weed pipes.

After Keyshore left Strait-laced smoke shop on Brown Street, he headed to the barbershop on V. Odom.

It felt so different now since his grandmother had passed, and not to mention, Rusty had been gunned down right in front of the shop.

Keyshore parked in the same parking space that Rusty was killed in, made sure he had his gun on his hip, then got out of his truck and entered the barbershop.

As he waited to get his hair cut, he and Miss Brooks sent some loving texts back and forth. Miss Brooks really didn't want to go on a trip because of the Covid-19 pandemic, but Keyshore had charmed her, and she gave in.

After K. Rock finished cutting his hair, Keyshore decided it was best that he went home and got well-rested. Their flight left at six in the morning, so there was no sense in being in the streets. Besides, he wanted to free his mind.

***

The next day, at about 4:15 a.m., Keyshore was

up and packing his things in a suitcase. He really wasn't taking much—he planned on buying a lot of new things on his trip. After he smoked a blunt, he jumped in the shower, then got dressed.

Miss Brooks met him at the Cleveland Hopkins airport around five-thirty, and they still had about a half hour before their flight left, so they decided to have breakfast together in the food court.

Keyshore couldn't stop cheesing, and Miss Brooks loved the attention and attraction he always showed.

When they landed in L.A., Miss Brooks was amazed by the scenery. She had never been out West, and with just the mental picture of all the snow she just left, she couldn't believe how beautiful it was in California.

She held tightly onto Keyshore's arm as they waited for the rental car he reserved to pull up. The sight of palm trees gave her such a tropical feeling, and she knew she could get used to that real quick.

When the valet pulled up and got out, he tossed the key to Keyshore; the key to a 2020 Bentley truck.

Keyshore looked Miss Brooks in the eyes, then kissed her on the forehead and told her, "This trip is all about you, my love."

A tear of joy dropped down Miss Brooks' face as Keyshore opened her side of the door to let her in.

He got in the driver's seat, then told her for the first time he loved her and wanted to spend the rest of his life with her. They kissed each other passionately, and the lust for sex bubbled in both of their systems.

The moment they entered their hotel room, clothes flew everywhere.

Keyshore laid her on the king-sized bed full of rose petals, kissing and licking slowly down her body. When he got to her pussy, he gently licked it once, then blew on it.

That drove Miss Brooks wild.

He sucked and kissed his way between her inner thighs, and worked all the way down to her toes, which he kissed, sucked, and rubbed. He then worked his way back to her pussy, slowly kissing it and allowing his tongue to swivel up and down, back, and forth, very slowly.

As Miss Brooks moaned with approval, Keyshore ran his tongue in and out of her pussy, kissing and sucking at it gently. He had full control and he knew it; every time Miss Brooks was close to orgasm, he would switch into a different pleasing format.

He finally decided it was time to allow Miss Brooks to cum, so Keyshore's tongue went to work, dancing back and forth on her clit until she orgasmed all over his tongue and lips.

His hard, nine-inch dick was now talking, and Miss Brooks went straight for it, sucking and licking it like it was meat on a bone.

She deeP.T.hroated him the farthest she could go, and Keyshore's eyes rolled into the back of his head from the fantastic dick-sucking she put on him.

He felt his self about to cum, so he pulled his dick out her mouth.

But Miss Brooks quickly grabbed and put it back in.

She looked up at him and purred, "I want you to cum in my mouth first."

Keyshore's body tensed up, and before the words could get out of his mouth, nut shot all into Miss Brooks' mouth and she swallowed every drop.

Not even a minute later, there was a knock at the door. Keyshore and Miss Brooks looked at each other in shock, and he put a finger to Miss Brooks, signaling for her to not say a word.

He quietly walked over to the door and looked through the peephole. He had to laugh at himself when he saw room service with the special meal, he had paid to be prepared for Miss Brooks an hour after they checked in.

Keyshore opened the door, and two chefs rolled

in the meal with a bottle of fine wine. When the chefs set the table with seafood everywhere, Miss Brooks, looking on from the sheets she was wrapped in on the bed, couldn't help but be impressed.

The chefs then lit the candles, poured two glasses of wine, and left.

Miss Brooks unwrapped herself from the sheets, and Keyshore carried her to the dinner table. Once he sat her in her seat, he prepared her plate and fed her.

After dinner, they went back to making love and enjoying each other for the rest of the night.

***

The next day, they were up early, and Keyshore took Miss Brooks shopping. They also went to the beach and had a picnic in the sand. Keyshore did a little surfing, although he wasn't good at all. They walked the shoreline of the ocean, holding hands and allowing the currents from the waves to hit their feet.

Miss Brooks really enjoyed both the trip and the attention Keyshore gave her.

They visited Beverly Hills, Hollywood, and a few resorts over the week that they spent in L.A. Miss Brooks loved the luxury, the scenic sights, and the stars and celebrities they bumped into. She got a real nice tan, too, seeing as it was winter back in Ohio. Keyshore took her to the movies, on the set, bungalows, and the list went on.

On their last day, they did a little more shopping. Keyshore bought so much stuff for them that he had to pay to get it delivered to Akron. Miss Brooks really made him happy, and he was ready to make her his woman—and maybe even his wife.

As they drove back to their room to get dressed for a beach party that night, Keyshore asked Miss Brooks to be his woman.

Miss Brooks smiled and replied, "I thought I already was your woman?"

Keyshore laughed, then said, "I just wanted to make it official."

He also asked Miss Brooks how she felt about living together, and when she said it would be great, sparks of happiness flooded his body. He told her about his friend Rod, and how having his house built from the ground up made him want to do that for them.

Miss Brooks smiled and had to remind Keyshore that he told her more than once that Rod had a house built from the ground up and that she would be flattered if they did the same.

They partied hard at the beach party that night, got really drunk, and almost missed their flight the next day. Keyshore was in love, and all he thought about was being with Miss Brooks as they flew back to Ohio.

CHAPTER 13

Joy is Pregnant

This was the third day in a row that Joy woke up and started throwing up, so she grabbed the pregnancy test she bought from the store and ran to the bathroom to piss on it.

About two minutes later she looked, and her heart dropped—she was pregnant.

Joy dropped the kit and started crying. She couldn't believe it. She didn't know if she was happy or mad—never in her life had she considered having a baby.

How was she going to tell Lil' Mark? How would he take it? A million thoughts raced through her head.

She got off the toilet, tossed the kit in the trash, washed her face, then brushed her teeth. She looked at herself in the mirror and just shook her head.

After she got out the shower, she figured it was only right to let Lil' Mark know, so she texted his phone to call her ASAP. She knew he was in Sioux Falls—a city in South Dakota—taking care of some legit business, so she didn't want to just call out of the blue.

Ten minutes later, the phone rang. It was Mark on the line.

He made her smile just hearing his voice—he was so great to her, and she was grateful. Lil' Mark asked if she was okay, because she was in a daze when he called, and she forgot to speak.

Joy apologized, then told Lil' Mark, "I am okay… besides the fact that I just took a pregnancy test and it told me I was pregnant."

"Yes, yes, yes!"

He was so happy to hear the news.

Joy smiled. She didn't think he would be this happy, but now she felt glad, too.

Lil' Mark started talking really loud, and he shouted, "I'm moving you and our baby down here, Joy! I was just deciding on buying this house, and now that I know you pregnant, it's as good as bought!"

Joy went silent. She was cool with having his child, but now she felt that he was moving too fast with the thought of moving them to South Dakota.

Lil' Mark sensed the silence and he asked Joy,

"What's wrong?"

Joy said, "Nothing!" but the truth was that she thought he was moving too fast.

Lil' Mark knew something was wrong, and somewhere deep down inside, he knew Joy didn't want to move.

After Joy hung up with Lil' Mark, she laid in bed and drifted into deep thoughts. Her life took on a lot of changes in such a short period, it seemed.

She had changed all her old phone numbers because L.X. kept sending threats. Word had gotten back to him that she was fucking Lil' Mark, and some people were saying Lil' Mark sent the hit on Young Ruler. But Keyshore informed him that Lil' Mark had nothing to do with the hit, so his name was cleared.

Joy was knocked from her thoughts when her 'money-phone' rang. She picked it up and made arrangements to meet her buyer at the gas station on East Avenue.

Joy pulled up to the gas station, went in, paid for her gas, and by the time she came out, her buyer, White Dan, was pumping her gas. White Dan was cool and very loyal to Joy—he always spent at least a thousand dollars every trip.

After he finished pumping her gas in the cold winter weather, he got in on the passenger side.

Today he bought a pound of ice, and Joy fronted him one, as well. Dan left the money in the side capsule like he always did, then grabbed the plastic shopping bag that laid on the floor of the passenger side.

And just like that he was gone, and she pulled off to make her money rounds.

After Joy finished making the sales she had lined up, she went and got her nails and toes done.

While she was getting her toes finished, Zeek texted asking her to meet him at his uncle's house. Joy cursed to herself—she forgot Zeek was out of ice and needed more.

She texted back, telling him to meet her at the trap.

When Joy pulled up to the trap, Zeek was already parked on the curve. She got out, grabbed a few bags she had from going to the store, then closed her car door.

Zeek grabbed the bags out of Joy's hand and followed her inside the house. Joy had to take a shit, and it was just Zeek's luck, because he was already in a hurry.

Zeek shouted, "Come on Joy, you going to make me miss my gapper, sis!"

Zeek paced back and forth in the living room, looking at his phone and texting, "I'm almost there," to his buyer.

He already had his money counted and laid on the table when Joy emerged from the restroom.

Joy had to laugh at the sight.

She shook her head and said, “Boy, you must be making a great profit with how you are acting!”

She was correct, too—Zeek bought three pounds of ice, and he had a play for all three that would triple the amount he paid.

Joy gave Zeek the three pounds, then kissed her on the cheek and told her he loved her and would see her later. He raced out the house, phone to his ear, and drove off to get his gapper.

Joy gathered up the money off the table from Zeek, then counted everything she made for the day. After she finished, she locked up the trap and set the alarm and camera system.

She made sure she had her 40-cal pistol on her hip, then jumped in her car and headed back to the apartment that she and Lil’ Mark now shared downtown.

Zeek met with his two white customers at a run-down strip club on Main Street.

They purchased all three pounds of ice and asked if they could get a better deal if they bought more. He said he didn’t know; he would let them know, even though he did already know. Zeek always waited until they pulled off before he pulled out, too.

Although he had been dealing with them for

almost a year now, he still believed in an abundance of caution. After they left, he waited a few minutes, then he left.

When Zeek stopped at the light on Main Street and Waterloo Road, he couldn't believe who he saw through his tinted windows.

It was Red Dawg, Young Ruler's main man and the voice of one of the niggas that Zeek remembered hearing when he was kidnapped.

Red Dawg was pumping gas and a dark-skinned young lady was driving the car he looked to be in.

When the light turned green, Zeek was so upset he was in the turning lane opposite of the gas station, but he quickly turned and pulled into the gas station across the street from the BP gas station that Red Dawg was at.

Time was on Zeek's side as he turned around to come right back out of the gas station. He ended up pulling a car behind the car Red Dawg was in.

Zeek quickly called Joy and told her he was on Red Dawg's tail. He let her know that it seemed like they were headed towards the Summit Lake apartments.

Joy began putting back on the clothes she just took off back on, grabbing her gun, and running out of the house all in the same motion, it seemed. She wasn't going to miss the chance to shoot Red Dawg in the face.

Zeek tried to hang up, but she made him stay on the phone with her as she pulled out in a rental car Lil' Mark kept just for these kinds of situations.

Zeek's assumP.T.ions was correct as the young girl's car pulled into the Summit Lake apartment complex. Zeek parked at the bottom of the parking lot when they parked at the top—he didn't want to draw any suspicion.

He watched Red Dawg get out the passenger side, and he could tell he had an extender clip on the gun he had by looking at the bulge from his hip. Red Dawg looked around really quick, then followed the dark-skinned young lady into her apartment.

Joy pulled up five minutes after Red Dawg went in and parked next to Zeek, but facing the opposite way. Zeek told her not to get out of her car, because he wasn't sure if Red Dawg had soldiers on the lookout—which, he did.

After about ten minutes went by, the two young Blood niggas Red Dawg had posted at an apartment a few doors down noticed that nobody got out of the two tinted-windowed cars at the end of the parking lot.

They didn't want to bother Red Dawg with it, so they decided to check it out themselves.

Zeek notice the two Bloods coming out from a

door a few doors from where Red Dawg went in.

He told Joy, “Pull off,” and he pulled off behind her.

The two young Bloods walked to the corner, then came back. They assumed it was probably some niggas stalking their baby mamas who were most likely getting fucked by someone else.

They laughed, dapped each other, then headed back to their post.

Zeek told Joy to meet him on Victory Street, where he owned a house that he was fixing up. When Joy parked behind him in the driveway, he got out.

Joy was so pissed.

Zeek told her, “Don’t be mad, we got him. And if his fuckboys thought it was an enemy, they would have shot!”

Joy had to think about it, and it *did* make sense... but she knew that in order to get him, they would have to creep on foot.

Time was ticking, and this opportunity wasn’t something that would come every day.

Zeek was already on the phone with his homeboy, Big Phil, who was notorious in the Summit Lake apartments.

Once Zeek got to talking big money, Big Phil was all in. He told Zeek he knew exactly which apartment Red Dawg was in and that the two dudes he kept on watch were some dusty, broke niggas, and Joy agreed to give Big Phil five bands if he made sure they got a good shot on Red Dawg.

Zeek left his car parked and jumped in with Joy.

Big Phil had them meet him at the apartments across Lakeshore Boulevard. Zeek pulled in the back, and Big Phil and two of his dudes were standing back there with black hoodies on. Big Phil ran down the game plan, and everyone dispersed in their assigned directions.

Big Phil sent his dudes to smoke a blunt and drink a bottle with Red Dawg's fuckboys, and he knew Red Dawg would come out for him if he wanted to buy coke.

Zeek and Joy would wait on the side of the building until Big Phil gave the code word, "Boyee."

Big Phil and his dudes headed to their three positions. Big Phil wasn't letting that free five-thousand get away from his hands, and it was all he thought as he walked across the streets. It was a cold world, and "murder bout money" was always the code to the streets of Akron.

Joy was ready to kill, and she couldn't *wait* to blow Red Dawgs brains out. Zeek was calm, but the killer was in him—in a way more major way than Joy. He had been putting in work since he was ten years old and caught his first body by twelve.

Big Phil was a man of his word, so Zeek knew today was going to be a killing, and it was up to them to make sure it was done right.

"Show no love—love will get you killed! Show no fear—fear will get you killed!" Those words played in Joy's head over and over as she waited for the moment.

Big Phil's dudes went into the flock apartment where Red Dawg's little Blood homies sat at a table facing the parking lot, passing a *Newport 100* cig back and forth.

They all knew each other and the dirty girl that stayed there, so it wasn't any suspicion, but Phil's dudes fired up a blunt, which brought the two Bloods into the living room. They dapped each other, and the blunt went into rotation along with a bottle of liquor.

Big Phil knocked on the dark-skinned young lady's door, where Red Dawg was at. Red Dawg answered from the top window.

Big Phil shouted, "Get out the pussy and bring me two grams—and it better not be cut!"

Red Dawg laughed and replied, "Come on Big Phil, you know I got gas!"

Red Dawg feared Big Phil. Anyone else, he wouldn't have served at night *or* without his two soldiers on deck, but he always got up any time of the night for Phil. Plus, Big Phil was bold as hell, and would knock until he did.

Red Dawg came outside, Phil handed him the money, and he gave Phil the dope all in one handshake-hug motion.

Big Phil then shouted, “Boyee! That pussy got you whipped, nigga!”

Red Dawg laughed, and before he could say, “no, it doesn’t,” Zeek and Joy appeared.

“What’s up now, nigga?!” Zeek shouted.

Joy shot first, hitting him right in the head, and Big Phil spun around, walking off like nothing ever happened.

Zeek followed up Joy with two shots that hit Red Dawg in the chest. Like wild wolves, they stood over Red Dawg emptying their clips, then ran off.

By the time Red Dawg’s little Blood homies heard the shots, it was too late. When they ran outside, all they saw was two hooded dudes running through the apartment towards Lakeshore.

They ran down to where Red Dawg was, and pain shot through their hearts. There were so many bullets in Red Dawg—the sight was unreal.

The dark-skinned woman he was fucking with came out when she saw the little homies, and she screamed, crying at the sight of Red Dawg stretched out. Big Phil’s two dudes walked over, too, just to see what they already knew.

By the time Joy and Zeek made it to Zeek's car, Big Phil was leaning on it and waiting for his pay. Joy tossed him the stack of money, then jumped in the car as Zeek pulled off smoothly.

Zeek dropped himself back off at his vehicle, and Joy jumped into the driver's seat, they went their separate ways in silence.

As Joy drove home, it felt crazy—she hadn't killed in over a year, almost, and here she was, pregnant and back killing people in cold blood.

When Joy got in the house she got undressed, took a shower, washed, and dried her clothes, then got in bed. She texted Lil' Mark and told him she missed him and couldn't wait until he returned home. Lil' Mark texted back he missed her too, and that he was so excited she was having his baby.

They sent love texts back and forth all night until Joy fell asleep.

CHAPTER 14

Akron Boyz in North Dakota

Marshall had Bismarck, North Dakota on smash—his restaurant was even doing *better* through Covid-19.

Lil' Mark sent Skelton and Goldie up his way while they were on the run, but Goldie knocked up a girl from Fargo three months after they arrived. Goldie felt it was a better mix for them in Fargo, so he and Skelton went there to get money.

The Akron Boyz had the state of North Dakota on smash; they had Fentanyl, Crystal Meth, and Perk thirties all flooded.

But Skelton ended up leaving Goldie in Fargo and taking his hustle to Mandan on 2nd Avenue. Goldie was cool with it—he loved Fargo, and since Skelton went to Mandan, he decided to move from 19th Avenue to Main Avenue.

Lil' Mark and Keyshore left Marshall in charge,

so the re-up always came through him, and so did the money.

Today, Marshall had a fresh shipment in, and everybody was happy that it finally came. A load of shit had got knocked off in the mail, and that left them on hold for two months. They all managed to make what they *did* have last up until about three weeks ago, so until today, shit had been fucked up for three whole weeks.

Marshall had Skelton and Goldie meet him in Williston to grab their loads. They all had to meet there regardless, because that's where the pack landed, anyways.

After everything was divided between the three of them, everyone went their own way with few words spoken.

Marshall had an old couple—a white man and white woman—driving an all-white van taking his pack to Bismarck, and Goldie had his girl and her sister driving his.

Skelton drove his own shit; he had a fake ID and a whole new identity in general that stated he was legit with a license as a car dealer.

But they all always made sure they let each other know when they touched safe to their destinations. So, like clockwork, everyone let it be known that they were safe when they landed.

The next day, Goldie pulled up on 19th Avenue

in his all-black Dodge Ram truck to serve his young dude, Little Mike-Mike. After he left from Little Mike-Mike, he met his homegirl, Hope, at the gas station.

Just the two sales put forty-thousand in cash in his pocket. He made sure he cut his circle to those two only after Skelton decided to trap in Mandan.

A lot of hustlers in Fargo were mad at Little Mike-Mike and Hope because of their loyalty to some out-of-town dudes, but reality was reality, and the out-of-town dudes had the best and cheapest drugs.

Mike-Mike was happy Goldie only fucked with him and Hope—not to mention, Skelton wasn't around anymore. He was doing good with his shipment, but when shit went dry three weeks ago, he had been in a panic. He had just spent big on a new Benz truck and rented a nice house for his girl and son, so seeing Goldie today put dollar signs back in his eyes. Goldie even fronted him what he bought, so he knew it was *super* on again.

Mike-Mike went right to work. As soon as the pack hit his hand, he was setting up a drug deal.

The ten pounds of ice he had were gone within that same day. Hope had all the good customers on the Fentanyl, so it took him longer than it would take her, but the perk thirties did about the same for both. Mike-Mike had perk thirties houses on every side of town, so after he bagged his pills up, he made stops at all the pill houses he ran.

Skelton had Mandan going crazy on 2nd Ave at his car dealership business, where he sold cars and you got it the "Big Drugs!" way.

Today, his customers weren't just buying cars—they were buying drugs to go with the cars. Skelton had his monopoly set up so smooth; he only sold his shit in the bulk amount, and you had to buy a used car to go with them every time you purchased.

He posted "big sale today!" on the billboard that sat in front of his car business. With him being out of drugs for three weeks, he knew today would be a good and busy day.

People came from all over North Dakota to spend with Skelton, but most came from right there in Mandan. By the time it was closing time, Skelton sold eleven used cars with drug buyers and seven used cars with random people.

He had to smile at himself as he sat at his desk in his office, counting thousands of dollars.

Marshall held shit down his way like he been doing for years. You couldn't tell him shit; he ran North Dakota with an iron-fist. Everybody from everywhere knew Marshall—his name rang bells all through North *and* South Dakota, but he really stopped serving people in North Dakota and let Goldie and Skelton run it up. Plus, he liked to overcharge, and South Dakota niggas never gave him no lip talk about his prices or quality.

Marshall's bag was gone in about three days tops this time, and he wasn't mad at the take at all. He knew that by the time his customers came back, Lil' Mark would have a much bigger load coming.

Lil' Mark had already told him "The motherload" was dropping a week after the one they had just received, and his job was to supply Goldie and Skelton when they ran out.

Lil' Mark himself was in Sioux Falls, South Dakota the whole time the shipments were dropping. Once his cousin Marshall sent word that the first load dropped, he had Keyshore get the big load enroute to land the next week.

After he and Keyshore had lost a big shipment sent to Bismarck, they both decided it was best for Lil' Mark not to be too far when shit dropped.

The route to Williston was a success, but they needed the motherload to land safe in Sioux Falls.

Lil' Mark was happy Joy was having his baby, and although he had a major move in play in Sioux Falls, he already had real estate there, too. He had his eye on a dream house—he wanted him and Joy to live there when he got out the game. Once she broke the news that she was having his baby, he bought the house.

However, Joy didn't seem too thrilled to move. Joy thought he was down here on some legit business, but the truth was not all-the-way truth.

Lil' Mark sat in his rental car at a food-packaging truck shipment company that one of Marshall's friends owned. He watched as an eighteen-wheeler pulled in and the workers went to work, unloading the truck and separating the shipments on the dock.

After the truck was emptied, it left its rig and picked up another rig that was loaded with packaged food in boxes. Everything was going smooth so far; now the next task was deliverance to Marshall's restaurant in Bismarck.

The workers quickly reloaded another eighteen-wheeler with the product and other restaurant food that Marshal ordered, and just like that, the shipment was off to Marshal's restaurant.

Lil' Mark pulled off a minute later, heading to Bismarck for a surprise visit with the package.

The eighteen-wheeler backed up in the back of Marshall's restaurant, and Marshall was front and center to help unload the shipment on the back dock. He and his workers worked quickly as they emptied all the food packaging out of the eighteen-wheeler.

By the time Marshall was pulling the last boxes off, Lil' Mark was standing on the side.

Marshall was a little startled at first, but once he recognized it was Lil' Mark, he winked and smiled at him. Everything went smoothly, and while Lil' Mark was glad, he was so ready to get back to Joy in Akron, Ohio.

But Lil' Mark wasn't missing a chance to eat his favorite meal in his cousin's restaurant. After they talked for a few hours and checked all the product delivered, Lil' Mark sat at a table and ate his favorite meal.

The next morning, he was in the sky, heading home to Akron and his new baby-mama-to-be, Joy.

Marshall was back to work, and things really went well for him. He decided it was best for him to start franchising his restaurant, so he opened a *Marshall's* in Fargo, Williston, and Mandan, North Dakota. Marshall was a hustler, but he was even better at business in the legit field. His little cousin Mark really put him in a better position, and now at a millionaire stage, his mind was telling him to get out of the game after this go around.

***

Skelton hung up the phone with Marshall. He was happy to hear that the motherload had dropped, and he could get whatever he could handle. He had made arrangements to meet with Marshall tomorrow, and he let him know he was sending his repo men to repossess a car so they could load it up.

After Skelton pulled out from his car lot, he headed to his town house to get ready for a hot date. He still couldn't believe that the beautiful mixed woman he met a few weeks ago allowed him a chance.

If only she knew he was a man wanted for a triple homicide...

Skelton took a nice, hot shower, and turned off all his business phones. There was no hustling going on tonight.

By about nine o'clock p.m., Skelton was dressed to impress, smelling good, and feeling even better. He tucked his gun on his hip, then left his house.

The beautiful mixed woman he met—named Jada—looked even better as she climbed in the passenger side of his 2021 Tahoe when he came to pick her up.

Jada was feeling the whole view of Skelton; she couldn't believe he was pushing a brand-spanking-new Tahoe—he looked like some real money.

Skelton pulled off once Jada was settled in her seat.

First, he took her to the movies, then they went bowling, and after that, they went to the new restaurant his homeboy Marshall owned.

The food was great, and Jada was really feeling Skelton—he moved around the restaurant like he owned the place.

After they ate, he went in the back and came back with a bottle of fine, white wine and two wine glasses. They both laughed and talked until the whole bottle of wine was empty.

Jada was really feeling good, so she asked Skelton, "Do you have any weed to smoke?"

Skelton had to laugh.

He told her, "You don't look like the type to smoke weed."

Jada laughed with him and said, "There's a lot that I do that I might not *look* like I do."

Skelton and Jada rode around, smoking a few blunts, talking about life and things they wanted to achieve.

Finally, he pulled up to the house he had picked her up from and parked. They sat in the car, still talking, and watched as people came and went from a house that must have sold drugs.

Jada reached over, then kissed Skelton on the

lips, and she thanked him for the nice time he showed her. She also told him that she was looking forward to seeing him again.

Skelton got out and walked her to her door, they kissed and hugged each other goodbye, and then he left.

***

Goldie was feeling good. He was on his third perk thirty, and second fifth of Hen. It was three a.m., and he was out being a hoe.

Lately, the perk thirty was becoming the drug of his choice—not to mention the fact that he could fuck two or three women off them.

He laid in his hotel room with five different women running around naked. Two women were lost in lust as they kissed each other in the hot tub, and the whole room smelled like exotic weed.

Goldie was getting some of the best head a man could ask for; every woman in the room took turns sucking his dick. But he refused to fuck any of them, which lead them to pleasing each other in sexual acts.

As long as Goldie had Mike-Mike and Hope holding it down, there wasn't much else for him to do.

When Goldie finally got home, it was eight a.m. the next day, and the moment he walked in the house, Janet was up in his face.

She was really getting tired of the disrespect, and him thinking money would solve the bullshit he did.

Janet was down for Goldie, but it wasn't about the money—even though Goldie thought she didn't know—she had seen Skelton and Goldie's faces on the America's Most Wanted website.

She had suspected a lot was wrong when she first met Goldie; his fake ID didn't match his name on Google, so she looked up fugitives on America's Most Wanted website, and bam—there was perfect pictures of Skelton and Goldie.

She had made it her business to get them better names and IDs with people that would never send red flags, and that was the reason they had lasted this long.

As Janet punched and slapped at Goldie, he grabbed her hands. He started kissing her, apologizing, and telling her he fell asleep at the trap on 19th.

She knew he was lying, because she pulled up to every place he hustled, and his truck was never there.

"Stop lying to me all the time, Goldie!" Janet screamed as he held her from hitting him.

Goldie gently kissed her lips, then started sucking on her neck. Once he heard her moan, he really went to work.

Before they knew it, he had her bent over the couch, making her pussy cum back-to-back as he put his stroke down. He really knew how to please Janet, but she hated how he controlled her with sex.

Goldie knew he was becoming addicted to the perk thirties. He had to stop popping, but he *needed* to at the same time.

Janet could sense something was wrong with him the next day. His body had the shakes, he was grouchy, and sweating way too much.

Goldie didn't give a fuck—he made his mind up that popping perks was over with.

It took him weeks to get the meds out his body, but like he promised himself, he did. Goldie vowed that he would never again use drugs he sold.

Hope finished her last sale, and after she left her homegirl, she headed to Mike-Mike's trap. She gave him the money for the Fentanyl she'd gotten from him when she was out, and they both decided to reup with Goldie at the same time.

But Hope had seen a lot of weakness in Goldie, and she promised herself that she would find out who his connect was.

CHAPTER 15

The West vs Raid

Roscoe-Cee pulled into a long driveway that sat deep up in the mountains of West Virginia. Lately he had been getting money with a big hillbilly named "John-Boy."

Business was good; John-Boy knew a lot of people that used ice and sold it. So far, Roscoe-Cee's luck on the highway had been good, and he made trip after trip from West Virginia to Akron.

After he met John-Boy in a trap he had in Charleston, John-Boy convinced him it was better to hustle from up in the mountains; a lot of out-of-town dudes hustled in the cities of West Virginia, so a lot of the cities were hot.

Roscoe-Cee parked the old F-150 truck he drove, got out, then moved a few old items he kept as a front. Up under an old air conditioner laid a plastic bag full of ten pounds of ice. He grabbed the bag, then headed to the house, where John-Boy already stood in the door open waiting for him.

They wasted no time. Within five minutes they were at the table busting down pounds of ice and getting ready for sales. There was no phone service in the mountains, so John-Boy did all house calls to his customers.

Roscoe-Cee had no worries; he always let John-Boy handle all the transactions. The flip was triple for him every time, and John-Boy made his profit in that same token.

Once every pound was broken down and rewrapped, John-Boy was out the door on a money mission. He came and went all day until there was roughly a pound and an ounce left.

As they sat counting money, Roscoe-Cee knew he needed to find a route to get more ice into West Virginia. Too many trips back and forth was becoming dangerous—he had already been pulled over one time with ten pounds in the truck. He was lucky the police missed it when they searched.

The next day, John-Boy was up and out the door before Roscoe-Cee woke up. He headed to his friend Harrison's house to see what was going on.

When he got there, everyone in the house was

high and had been up for days. John-Boy grabbed one of the pipes and put some ice on it, then started smoking it. He got everyone high for free this time, because they always spent money with him.

After he left Harrison's house, he met his power customer, who bought the rest of the ice from him. John-Boy made off well every time, and always managed to save himself at least an ounce to smoke and party with for free.

When John-Boy pulled back up to his house, he noticed things scattered all around inside and outside of Roscoe-Cee's truck.

Somebody was searching around on his property, because John-Boy knew Roscoe-Cee didn't get up until at least noon.

He quickly raced into his house, and just as he thought, Roscoe-Cee was asleep on the couch. John-Boy went back outside, looking around with his shotgun in hand, but nobody was in sight.

He checked the dirt road and noticed different car tracks in the dirt.

Something wasn't right, so he put all of Roscoe-Cee belongings back into his truck and headed back into the house.

Roscoe-Cee woke up at about noon like always and noticed John-Boy sitting in the rocking chair across from him. Roscoe-Cee grabbed his pack of cigarettes off the table and a lighter, and he lit a cigarette for himself.

John-Boy looked up at Roscoe-Cee and asked him, “Did you hear anybody outside?”

Roscoe-Cee looked puzzled.

He took another drag from his cigarette, then said, “No! Was I supposed to be expecting someone? Because I was knocked out.”

John-Boy explained to him how he’d seen all the things from the back of his truck scattered everywhere.

Roscoe-Cee was still confused, but John-Boy continued explaining to him that someone was searching through his truck. He also informed him that he spotted tire tracks that he’d never noticed before in his dirt-road driveway.

“Well,” Roscoe-Cee said, “the good thing is, we don’t have nothing left, because I’m sure you sold the rest.”

Although Roscoe-Cee was correct about him selling the rest and the house being clear, John-Boy didn’t like the feeling he was getting.

But they counted the money John-Boy made earlier that day, then separated the differences, and Roscoe-Cee put the rest of the money in an old book bag he had already with money in it.

John-Boy decided it was best for them to wait a few days before they did anything else—just to make sure no police were snooping around.

Roscoe-Cee agreed, and felt it also was best that he moved the money.

Roscoe-Cee left John-Boy's house and headed back to Akron after he let John-Boy know he would be back by the weekend.

When he got on the highway, so did an unmarked federal car.

Roscoe-Cee made it back to Akron safe—or so he thought. The whole time, he was being watched, and he didn't notice.

When he went into his house, the federal agent put a tracking device on his truck, took a few pictures, then left.

Roscoe-Cee couldn't wait to lay in his bed, but his daughter wasn't having that. She attacked her father as soon as he came through the door, asking question after question, demanding he see this and that.

By the time his daughter tired out, he was even more exhausted than before.

He jumped in the shower and enjoyed the hot, steamy water for about fifteen minutes, and when he got out, the smell of food being cooked was in the air.

"What a great baby mother..." he sighed to himself.

Back in the mountains of West Virginia, the feds stormed John-Boy's home. He saw them coming as car after car pulled up in his driveway.

"Search Warrant! Search Warrant!" the feds screamed as they knocked hard on his door.

John-Boy flushed the eight-ball of ice he had left, then opened the door.

"On the ground!" the officers shouted as they rushed in.

John-Boy was furious as he watched them ransack his home.

Room after room, they shouted, "clear!" as there wasn't anyone else there or any drugs in the home.

Two federal agents sat John-Boy in a chair at his home and began questioning him. John-Boy refused to speak or answer any of the questions they asked.

Next, they came with pictures of Roscoe-Cee, his truck, and the home in Akron. John-Boy still refused to say a word, but when they came with the controlled buys they had on him, shit changed.

His friend Harrison had been setting him up the whole time—he couldn't believe it.

The feds realized they finally broke into John-Boy, Mr. Tough-guy Personality, and they quickly went to work.

"Save yourself, John-Boy!" the head federal agent urged him, "We already know it's the black kid from Akron bringing the drugs—we just don't have any buys on him."

John-Boy shook his head no; he couldn't do it.

Roscoe-Cee got up early the next morning—he had a lot of running around to do. He met with Lil' Mark on Manchester Road at the new trap, and they counted the money he owed and was spending.

Lil' Mark had to give it to Roscoe-Cee; he was getting business done in West Virginia like he promised he would.

They sat around, smoking a few blunts, just talking and building on how to get a big load into West Virginia as two federal agents drove by the trap very slowly. They wrote down the rental car tag number and took pictures of the house, Roscoe-Cee's truck, and the rental car.

Lil' Mark happened to look at his surveillance camera just then, catching a white man and a black man taking pictures from a white impala. He raced towards the door to see why, but they were gone.

"Fuck!" Lil' Mark shouted.

He went into panic. He knew that the police—or feds—were on one of their asses. Roscoe-Cee caught the vibe and was getting nervous himself.

"We gotta get up out of here," Lil' Mark shouted, "and leave that truck!"

Lil' Mark was built ready; he kept a spare car

always parked two blocks away from his trap.

He tossed Roscoe-Cee an all-black hoodie and they quickly left out the back door and strapped a book bag full of money on his back with his pistol on his hip.

Once they made it to the spare car safely, Lil' Mark made sure Roscoe-Cee left his phone broken into pieces.

As Lil' Mark pulled off, he decided he wanted to drive past the trap to see if anything unusual happened.

He drove past slowly. Everything looked the same, but he knew the cops when he saw them. He grabbed a spare phone from the glove compartment, and texted Keyshore, "911-221."

Keyshore texted "V. Odom," and Lil' Mark headed to the barbershop to meet him.

When Lil' Mark and Roscoe-Cee pulled up, Keyshore was standing in the driveway, talking on his phone. He hung up when he saw Lil' Mark parking. Roscoe-Cee stayed in the car while Lil' Mark and Keyshore spoke.

Lil' Mark informed Keyshore of what happened and every move he made afterwards. Keyshore had to smile; Lil' Mark was sharp on his feet and thought quick in serious situations.

"That was definitely the police," Keyshore assured him.

They needed to clean the spot out as quick as

possible, so Keyshore sent a few of his cool white dudes to clean the job.

Lil' Mark said there was only like five pounds of ice and a few pounds of weed left in there, so Keyshore made sure it would make it to his hand.

Late that night, the whole trap and both vehicles went up in flames. Roscoe-Cee moved his family, and Lil' Mark and Joy moved their house as well.

"Better safe than sorry," was the motto Lil' Mark and Keyshore lived by, and little did they know that it was the smartest move so far.

That next morning, the federal agents assigned to the West Virginia raid were furious. They couldn't believe when they drove past the trap on Manchester Road—it was burnt down.

What could have happened? The tracker never showed the truck Roscoe-Cee drove leaving, but it stopped working late last night.

They decided to drive by Roscoe-Cee's family house only to get a big shock.

How the fuck could his house be empty? What, did he move at night?

The two federal agents sat in Roscoe-Cee's old driveway, lost for words.

***

Without John-Boy's cooperation, things were at a standstill.

John-Boy sat in his cell; he had no way to warn Roscoe-Cee, but he also had no means of snitching, either. The federal agents went to work on him for weeks, but he remained silent.

Eventually they had no choice but to charge him for the little they had, which only left him a guideline of fifteen to twenty-something months.

John-Boy ended up running into some young black dudes that knew Roscoe-Cee, and they got word to Keyshore. The shit made a lot of sense, so Keyshore made sure Roscoe-Cee took great care of John-Boy his whole federal jail time.

Roscoe-Cee's name was hot now, and the feds were watching him every time they could catch up with him. He decided to move to Canton, Ohio, get out of the game for a while, and just work. He knew they were on his ass, and he refused to get his team caught up in his bullshit.

One day when he was leaving work, two federal agents swooped up on him in the parking lot. They joked and talked shit to him—they warned him not to *ever* get back in the game, or they would surely get him.

The run-in with the feds really gave a different view to Roscoe-Cee. He wouldn't dare give them the chance to take him away from his family, so he made sure he let Keyshore knew every time he had contact with any officers of the law, even though he wasn't hustling anymore at the moment.

CHAPTER 16

Welcome Home Brain

Brain walked out the federal prison a free man. It had been ten long years straight, and he spent it getting his mind right spiritually and physically. Although he looked so innocent, he left a murderous name back home in Akron.

Keyshore blew the horn when he noticed Brain looking around to see where he was. He then got out of his 2021 BMW truck. Brain walked towards him with a big smile; it had been forever since they had been out of jail at the same time.

Keyshore shook his hand, then hugged him tight. He almost shed a tear—his little bro was free. Although they weren't blood-related brothers, you couldn't tell.

He opened the back door to the truck and grabbed the bags with clothes for Brain while he was already taking his jail clothes off, Keyshore was handing him his stuff.

It was a nice, hot summer day in July, and Brain was looking like a million bucks. He wore a polo Ferragamo shirt with some matching Ferragamo loafers, and casual shorts. The bust-down Rolex with John Ford glasses that Keyshore gave him set his swag off—and that was even before Keyshore informed him that the all-white BMW truck was his.

Brain drove the whole way back from New York to Akron, and Keyshore was so happy he did. He dropped Keyshore at home, grabbed the bands Keyshore had for him, then headed straight to get his kids.

He had made sure Keyshore kept him getting out as a secret, because he had a lot of unfinished business to take care of.

After he picked his daughter and son up, he jumped right back on the highway, and headed to Atlanta, GA.

He enjoyed the whole ride—his kids updated him on everything and told him everything they wanted him to buy. He couldn't believe that his daughter was a teenager now, and his son was ten already.

They pulled into a hotel in Atlanta late the same night. Tomorrow they had a big day, so they checked in and went right to sleep.

The next morning, everyone was up early and ready to hang out and shop. Brain took the kids to breakfast, then they hit “the underground” to shop, and he spent every bit of twenty-thousand shopping for clothes. Brian had bought so much stuff for them that he had to mail some of it home.

The three of them ate out, visited a few family members and friends, then chilled at the hotel to have some quality time. The whole weekend was theirs.

Sunday came fast, and they were back on the road, headed home to Akron. Brian felt good, too—he loved his kids so much. He vowed that nothing else would ever take him away from them again.

He dropped his daughter off first, because his relationship with his son’s mother was still active. By the time he reached his son’s mother’s house, his son was asleep, so he grabbed his son and took him in first, then grabbed the things he bought for him.

His baby mother was all over him after he finished setting everything down inside. They kissed and held each other tight, and before you knew it, they were in her bed making sweet love.

Brain woke up at about four a.m.; it was time to take care of business. He quickly got dressed in all black, made sure his guns were loaded and ready, then left the house.

Brain jumped on an old bike that was in his baby mother's backyard. He decided it was safe to move like he was just a young person riding a bike for exercising.

A young dude named "Hulk" from Detroit had been getting money in Akron for going on five years now, and nobody in the 'hood made it their business to address it. Brain couldn't believe the traffic that came and went from Hulk's trap house on Howe Street, and he couldn't believe Keyshore, Lil' Mark, or Roscoe-Cee hadn't addressed it either.

Brain walked his bike around back, and then walked right up to the front door with no mask on and knocked. Hulk answered the door off guard, because he had no problem with nobody in the Valley. As soon as the door opened, Brain pointed his gun and barged right in, smacking Hulk across the head—*hard.*

"Shut the fuck up!" Brain shouted at the two dope-fiend prostitutes that were laid on a mattress ass-naked.

He quickly yanked Hulk from off the floor and made him tie the two fiends up. After that, he dragged him to his safe and stash, and finished off by killing everyone in the house with clean shots to the head.

Brain took the back door out of Hulk's house, mainly because Hulk had a lot of traffic coming from crack and perk thirties sales; someone was already knocking on the front door as he left the back doorway with a book bag full of money and drugs.

He ignored the knock and ran out, jumping the fence in the backyard. He jumped back on his bike and rode off like nothing ever happened.

When he returned to his baby mother's house, it must have been about seven-thirty in the morning, and his son was up playing video games while his baby mom was cooking breakfast. Brain walked into the kitchen then smacked her on the ass before kissing the back of her neck.

She scolded him, "Stop Brain!" with a big smile on her face—she was so happy to have him home.

***

The 'hood was on fire—three dead bodies and nobody had seen anything or known anything about it.

The new lead homicide detective was Detective V05, and his reputation was on the line.

The name "V05" stuck with him from his police officer days; he was known to clean up any drug and crime area in the city. But now, his job was to solve all these unsolved murders in Akron.

He took notes and viewed all the areas in the house. From what he gathered, it wasn't a case of forced entry. Judging by all the things he noticed scattered around and the open, empty safe, this had been a robbery.

What he *couldn't* understand was why the robber killed everyone; it looked like they followed all his commands.

V05 felt anger welling up in him as he viewed the two women tied together, naked, and the young man laid out on the floor with his brains blown out and his pants pulled down to his ankles, pockets inside out.

***

That same day—but later that night—Brain was right back at it. This time, he took Keyshore along for the ride.

Word had gotten back to him about the niggas who killed Rusty, and Keyshore couldn't believe he was going on this mission—or even the fact Brain was already ready to kill fresh out of prison.

They rode in silence as they headed to a trap spot on the North side on Wall Street.

Keyshore couldn't believe his eyes when he saw the same black Tahoe that he had seen when Rusty was killed. Anger filled his system, and the urge to kill was back in him—just like that.

Brain had the whole rundown, and a dope-fiend prostitute was his way inside—which he was going to be sure to kill as well.

He parked down the street, gave the junkie two fifty-dollar bills, then sent her to cop.

Once she got the drugs, she hit 'send' on her phone's text, and Brain and Keyshore were right at the door when it open.

Brain shot her in the face first, then barged straight in, shooting the doorman. Keyshore was right behind him, and shots rang out from both of their guns.

By the time, the house was clear, four dead bodies laid spread out on the floor. Brain was rummaging through one of the dead men's pockets when Keyshore snapped out of it.

"Come on, bro! Let's go, nigga!" Keyshore hissed when he realized Brain was robbing the men.

They both shot out the back door, running through a few houses backyards until they reached where they had parked, and Brain drove off nice and smooth like nothing never happened.

Keyshore looked over at Brain, and all he could do was shake his head; he knew his little bro was a natural-born killer like himself.

"What happen to Demond?" Brain asked Keyshore when he caught him looking at him.

"I had to kill him, bro," Keyshore answered.

And that conversation never went any farther than that. They just rode back to Keyshore's truck in silence. Keyshore got out, and Brain pulled off.

Brain pulled up on the South side to address the cousin of a nigga he killed ten years ago, who couldn't seem to keep what he was going to do to him out of his mouth.

When he pulled on Cole Avenue, it was like taking candy from a baby. The dude was standing on the corner with three other dudes, laughing and talking shit.

Brain drove past, turned around, then parked about a block away. He threw his hood on over his face, and these young dudes *had* to be green, because they didn't seem to think it was odd or unusual for a man to be walking with a hood on his head in the summer of July.

He walked right up and shot the little nigga straight in the head, and his three friends took off running as soon as they heard the shots.

Brain stood over the lifeless body and shot him five more times before running back to his car and pulling off.

Brain had the city on edge—nobody knew who was doing all these killings, and all the hustlers were on pins and needles.

He made his first real appearance in the 'hood after the triple homicide he put down when he pulled up on Manchester Road to D.B.'s corner store to get a feel of the 'hood. Nobody was out, but after ten minutes, the parking lot began to fill.

He had all his young Cheste niggas everywhere; there were so many cars that any customers couldn't pull into park at the store.

Big bottles went around and weed smoke filled the air as Brain listened to groups after groups of his niggas giving him updates. Roscoe-Cee walked up, and Brain dapped, then hugged him.

But he could sense the defeat in Roscoe-Cee, and it hurt him deeply. Everything that Roscoe-Cee shared with him he already knew, but he respected his young nigga for his loyalty and the fact that Roscoe-Cee still managed to hand him a thousand dollars. As bad as Brain didn't want to acceP.T. it from him, he had to, in order to keep from hurting Roscoe-Cee's pride.

By the time Keyshore, Lil' Mark, and Rod pulled up, the Cheste was going crazy like it was a block party. They all decided it was best that they took the party down the street to Lane field, so everyone followed. Some drove and some walked, but the whole valley came together for Brain today, even though an 'up the way' and 'down the way' beef was cooking behind a few murders.

Keyshore was proud that everyone got along, and honestly, this was how he felt it *should* be. They gambled, barbecued, played basketball, played cards, danced to the music, and got drunk all the way until the police shut them down at eleven that night.

Keyshore parked the rental car he drove on Lacroix Street, then jumped into the BMW truck with Brain. They rode and talked for hours about the 'hood and rebuilding it all legitimately. A lot of people wanted to run the 'hood, but nobody wanted to buy back the 'hood and own all the property.

Things were bigger than them, and they both agreed it was time to make legit changes and create jobs and hope for the community. Who would ever think or believe such cold-hearted killers like them had such a strong intellect like they did?

With all the wrong they had done, they knew it was only right that they make it right for the community; it was time to teach the children what should have been taught to them. It was time to show the children that it was okay to be police officers, judges, lawyers, mayors, governors, and so on.

By the time Brain dropped Keyshore back off to his rental car, it was close to four in the morning, and Keyshore staggered to the car.

Brain shouted out, “Are you good to drive?”

Keyshore rolled down the window once he was in and let Brain know he was good, then pulled off. Still, Brain ended up following him until he pulled into the parking deck of his condo just to be safe.

***

The niggas on the East side had a lot of love for Brain, so he decided to pull up on his homeboy “Monster,” who just came home two days ago.

Monster was up early smoking “Za” over at the house of some little bitch he met and fucked the day he got out. Brain parked on Whitney Street, tucked his gun—and the gun he brought for Monster—then went in.

Monster opened the door as Brian walked up, and let him in. Brain handed him a new “FN” gun and about four thousand in cash. Monster tried to pass him the blunt in exchange, but Brain waved it off.

They sat and talked for about an hour and a half before Brain left to pick his daughter up.

Later that night, Brain was back on the East side, parked at the drive thru on Lovers’ Lane and talking with a few Blood niggas. They updated him about the situation with Joy, and how she had Young Ruler killed. They also informed him about how they thought that Lil' Mark put the play down for her, but they couldn't prove it.

Brain was all ears as he listened to the scoop and the politics of what went on while he was away, and he found out that there was a lot of beef in the air and a lot of killing going on. Around the corner of Sylvan Street, a movement had formed, and even the East side became sectioned off.

As Brain pulled off from Lovers' Lane, he couldn't believe his eyes.

A young kid, no older than twelve years old, ran up and shot another dude right in the head in his car at the drive thru. Brain scattered, and everyone else did the same.

Word later came that the older dude who got killed in his car had sold the twelve-year-old some fake drugs.

***

Akron was seeing a hot summer—not in weather, but murders. A funk was in the air, and the beef was being handled professionally.

After witnessing that twelve-year-old commit that murder in front of everyone, Brain knew that he had to stay on point *always*. Not to mention, word was out that he had money on his head for a murder he honestly hadn't committed.

Brain drove through the city just thinking and looking at his surroundings through his tinted windows. So much had changed, yet he was right back in the game like he never left.

The talks he had with Keyshore played in his mind repeatedly—it made so much sense for them to monopolize and really do it legit.

Covid-19 had the business economy fucked up, but like Keyshore assured him, there still was ways around that.

The goal was to buy all the houses, and buildings in the valley where they grew up at. As a team, everyone from the 'hood, had to at least buy one house in the 'hood to be a part of the movement.

Brain already had two, and now his eyes were on buying five more within the next three months.

CHAPTER 17

The Winter Hit, and Coke Came Back Around

Rod was deep in conversation with his Mexican lady friend. She was cussing and fussing him out, because he hadn't been down to see her in Texas since he been home. She was always coming to Ohio for him, and she was tired of his excuses.

"Niña!" Rod shouted as she went on and on bitching at him.

Right before Rod was about to hang up on her, her uncle walked in and grabbed the phone from her.

"Invierno! What can you do with that season?"

"Yo figura un poco de nieve, if that's what's needed," Rod informed him.

"Sí," her uncle responded.

And just like that, old-school coke was on its way to Akron by the bricks, and Rod decided he would cut Brain in on the coke movement since he was home now—but only if he wanted in.

His girl's uncle had two Mexicans drive all the way from Texas in a little-ass Honda with twenty bricks of coke. They pulled right into the 'hood five days after Rod spoke with his girl's uncle.

Twenty-five thousand a brick wasn't bad at all in this day and age. Coke was a hot ticket, and it barely came around, so Rod couldn't go wrong with the front.

Rod still ended up sending half the money he owed on the tab, even though he didn't have to, and Brain was game to get in on the coke connection, so Rod split the bricks in half with him and only charged him two bands extra off each brick.

The coke was so good that they turned each brick to a brick and a half, and it still was a ten. Rod and Brain was finished with the twenty bricks within two weeks, and the Mexicans were back to refill and pick up just as fast.

Rod was so flashy, rich, and young, and he didn't give a fuck, either. But a lot of people who didn't really know him had him misjudged; they thought that just because he had money his gangsta wasn't "G," which was just how he liked it. He was just as much a killer as the niggas that represented "Murder Bout Money."

Who knew what started making niggas he knew try him, but they did, and he was either killing or having them killed every time.

***

Keyshore pulled up to the Summit Mall to meet Miss Brooks, who was already parked and waiting as he parked next to her. They both got out and hugged each other, then proceeded into the mall, holding hands as they walked.

Miss Brooks and Keyshore made sure that at least one day out of every week, they had a date night. Today, Keyshore took her shopping, and there was no limit to what she could buy.

The love grew stronger every day, and Keyshore had a house that was being built from the ground up for them both, and he let her oversee everything. She had picked a nice piece of land out in Stow with an amazing view of a lake and woods.

Life was great for them, and Keyshore was living up to everything she asked of him. He knew he had to get all the way out the streets, but after the killings with Brain felt tied in.

Miss Brooks was everything in a woman he could ask for. They bought matching Polo suits and Airmax shoes, and she had so many bags that Keyshore had to make two trips to their cars.

At around nine p.m. they headed home.

Keyshore followed her to her house to drop her things off and park her car. Once they were done, she jumped in with him and they drove off into the night.

He got on the highway heading towards Cleveland, and they played the slow jams of the 90s all the way until he parked in The Grey Area food spot. When they got out to go in and eat, Keyshore reminded Miss Brooks that this was the place he brought her food from the first time they met.

She smiled and hugged onto his side even tighter as they walked in.

Tonight, Keyshore's homeboy—who owned the place—was in. S.Q. greeted Keyshore as soon as he looked up and saw him. He was draped in so much expensive jewelry that Miss Brooks thought he was a music rapper! But S.Q. and Keyshore shook hands, and he led the couple to a nice corner table in the back.

Once Miss Brooks got comfortable, Keyshore instructed her to place her order and said he would be right back and stepped outside to talk to his nigga S.Q..

The minute he came out, S.Q. was showing him his fleet of cars and *man* did he have some nice whips... Keyshore had to give him that.

They laughed and reminisced about the jail time they did in the past, and about fifteen minutes later, P.T. pulled up as if they had talked him up. Keyshore got so lost in his reminiscing that he forgot he had Miss Brooks still inside.

When he realized his mistake, he quickly cut their reunion short with promises of coming alone the next time.

By the time he made it back to the table, Miss Brooks was already enjoying her meal.

She smiled and told him, "I tried to wait for you."

Keyshore sat down and went right to work on his own plate. The food was great, and the night was still young in his mind. He still had a few surprises for Miss Brooks tonight, and like always, he was out to charm her.

S.Q. tossed Keyshore the keys to his yacht on the couple's way out the door. When Keyshore parked and led Miss Brooks towards the yacht's dock on Lake Erie, she couldn't believe it.

They had such a romantic night on the water that Keyshore fell in love with S.Q.'s yacht and vowed to purchase his own. He and Miss Brooks ended up staying the night in the yacht, making sweet love all night long, watching movies, and viewing miles of beautiful water.

The next morning, Keyshore dropped S.Q.'s keys off, then headed home to Akron. He took

Miss Brooks to breakfast, and then dropped her off at home. She thanked him and told him how much she enjoyed herself. She didn't understand how she deserved all the good treatment Keyshore gave her, but Keyshore always made sure she realized that she deserved it—and more.

***

Rod was really feeling himself as he looked at his reflection in the mirror. Rainbows glistened off his five chains, Rolex bust-down watch, bracelet, and pinky ring. This nigga had on a million dollars' worth of jewels—and between him and S.Q., he wasn't too far behind.

Rod had so much new money coming that he couldn't keep count. Although he put Brian in position, their view on the 'hood was totally different—he knew a 'hood war was about to blossom.

He was a super team-player type of guy, so it was always a human chess game with him. Keyshore loved them both—Brain was older than Rod, but they held a lot of the same qualities.

Rod tucked his gun in his Gucci pants, grabbed his keys to his SRT truck, and headed out the door to the 'hood. He had the Cheste flooded with every drug you could think of, and now the coke was back as well.

He really fronted his share of the coke to the OG's in the 'hood who just couldn't keep up with the new wave, and he made sure that everybody that ran with him got to eat.

To be honest, he really had more power in the 'hood than Keyshore, Lil' Mark, and Brain—mainly because he was the youngest and spent more time in the 'hood—but Rod respected the big homies, and everyone respected him. It wasn't a 'better-than-you' type of situation; it was a circle of well-respected niggas trying to bring wealth back into the 'hood and the whole city of Akron.

As soon as Rod parked on Lacroix Street at the new trap he'd opened, ten young niggas appeared, strapped and ready to kill if need be. He smiled at the sight of everyone being on cue, the youngest being only twelve years old, yet ready for whatever.

He jumped out, tossing his young nigga in charge a zip of "Za Za" to roll up as he headed to the porch.

Blunt after blunt went around, and Dolf peeked through the blinds, then tapped on the window for Rod to come talk to him. Dolf was older than Rod, but they were truly close, and Dolf was also on the run for all kinds of shit.

Rod grabbed the blunt took a puff, then got up to go inside the house. He listened to Dolf as he continued to puff on the blunt of "Za Za."

Dolf told him how the coke and crack was moving better than expected, even with Brain having a coke spot around the corner. But the Fentanyl was moving with no competition; "goldmine" was the only way to address that.

Keyshore had been on Rod's ass, so today he was making it his business to buy two houses in the 'hood. He bought one on Taylor Street, and one on Blanch Street.

"Keyshore is going crazy," Rod thought to himself.

But he respected the view about owning the 'hood legitimately and creating for "all of ours," even the ones not in the game.

Lil' Mark pulled up on Rod, and he seemed upset that Rod didn't cut him and Keyshore in with the coke plug.

But Rod stood his ground and put respect on his name as he explained to Lil' Mark that he felt Brain deserved a nice wave to himself.

Lil' Mark could do nothing but respect it, but he also informed him that there would be much more money if him and Brain pushed some of the bricks down to North Dakota. He also informed him that they still had Goldie and Skelton down there on the run.

Rod promised him that he would run that by Brain, because his say-so meant just as much.

Rod himself didn't mind at all, and he figured he could send Dolf down there, as well.

The valley was full of life as business transpired all through every street. Between Keyshore, Lil' Mark, and Brain, every street had a house selling something—not to mention the others in the 'hood who did their own thing, as well.

When Rod came to drop Brain his half of the bricks that came in, Brain was sitting at a table with eyes glued to a chessboard.

He and an old-school homie named "Grandad" were in a serious battle, and Brain was losing. Brain didn't even look up at Rod, he just told him to drop the bag by his side.

Rod stood and watched them play after he did what Brain instructed.

After about four more games, Brain finally gave up—plus he had the impression that Rod had something important to speak with him about, seeing how he still was standing there an hour later.

Brain told Grandad "Good games," and that he would catch up with him later. Grandad got up, then left out the door, laughing and talking shit all the way until he was outside.

Rod told Brain about the North Dakota wave, and how much more money they could make. Brain was cool with it because Goldie and Skelton were his little niggas anyways, and he knew they would do right by him.

Rod asked, "Do you think sending Dolf down there is a good idea?"

Brain gave him a cold look, reminding him how much he didn't care for Dolf. Rod caught on quick and decided he wouldn't send Dolf. It also reminded him that he would have to also keep Dolf and Brain out of the same room.

He cussed to himself because he'd forgot about the beef between them and what it was about. Now, he would have to clean the situation the best he could.

He went right to work, letting Brain know that Dolf was his dude and that he would appreciate if they didn't kill each other while in the 'hood. An alliance was agreed, and both parties put it on Wayne-G and Truck—may they rest in peace—to never break the alliance.

***

Psalms 109:26 was what Keyshore shouted as he awoke from a nightmare; "Help me, O Lord my God! Save me according to your steadfast love!"

The game was haunting him, yet God was forgiving him and welcoming him all in the same token.

***

Roscoe-Cee couldn't take it anymore. His baby mama's respect for him was dying by the day, his job wasn't paying the bills, and the niggas in Canton were testing his manhood.

As soon as he came in from work, his baby mother grabbed her coat and left him home with the kids. He didn't even have the energy to fight or ask where she was going, looking and smelling so good.

Once Roscoe-Cee's baby mama got in her car, she dialed the number of a Canton dude she met at the gas station. He was already looking out for her, and she had only been fucking him for a week.

She felt bad for doing it, but Roscoe-Cee just wasn't attracting her anymore. She pulled over at her new friend's apartment, parked, and went inside.

He wasted no time. They fucked and made love for two hours straight, and after they finished, she showered, got dressed, and took the money he gave her on the way out the door.

When she arrived home, Roscoe-Cee and the kids were all sleeping together in her bed. Tears rolled down her cheeks, but in her heart, she felt she was doing what she had to do to survive.

She ended up crashing on the couch, not disturbing the rest of her family.

The next morning, Roscoe-Cee was up early. He had a meeting with Brain, and something *had* to give; his gas tank was on E by the time he made it to Akron, and he only had twenty dollars to his name until he got paid the next week.

He told Brain everything, and today, he was letting him know that he couldn't continue living like this. Work wasn't getting it; he explained to Brain that hustling was all he knew.

Brain gave him the same thousand dollars he gave him when he first came home. He knew Roscoe-Cee was going through it, and as much as he wanted to put him back in the game, he couldn't—Roscoe-Cee was too hot.

But Brain was in the process of starting a cleaning service that would help him earn well—he just had to be patient.

Roscoe-Cee disregarded what Brain, Keyshore, and Lil' Mark asked of him. He took nine-hundred dollars of the thousand Brain gave him and purchased some weed to hustle in Canton. The hustler was in him, and he wasted no time getting to it.

***

Rod pulled back to his spot-on Lacroix Street—business was in full session. His niggas ran the trap like the mob; they sold every drug you could want.

Right now, he scrolled down his Instagram page, checking out what was going on around the city and the rest of the world. His Mexican lady texted him, so he texted her back and forth some, too.

When Dolf woke up from a "Za Za" coma, he was shocked to see Rod still hanging out this late.

"You must be about to cheat on your bitch tonight!" he said.

Even though he was right, Rod didn't let him know, and didn't even answer him back; the blunts just got rolled and passed around like always, and blunt after blunt was chain-smoked.

***

Brain drove down Lacroix Street. Although he made an alliance, he wanted to see if he caught Dolf outside anywhere around Rod's spots. But when he didn't catch sight of him anywhere, he continued onto his original route.

Rod did have it jumping up there, he had to admit.

He headed to the Southwest side to see what

was up with a few people he hadn't run into yet—Rod splitting the coke connect with him really put him up faster than expected, so he couldn't complain.

When he got on Lake Street, he parked and went inside to holler at his young bitch.

She screamed his name in delight as soon as she opened the store.

Brain went inside and went straight to business; he fronted her two ounces of coke and gave her a .22 pistol to protect herself.

She already had customers, but he let her know that he would be sending some customers to her as well.

CHAPTER 18

It's A Girl

Joy screamed, "Help me, Lil' Mark!"

Her water had just busted, and it felt like the baby was coming.

Lil' Mark raced into the bathroom to help Joy off the toilet.

"Oh my god!" he shouted.

The baby was trying to come!

Lil' Mark was in full panic mode, but he decided it was safe for him to call the ambulance. He quickly dialed 911, and within eight minutes the ambulance was outside, and paramedics were coming in.

They put Joy on the stretcher, then raced her to the hospital, where she gave birth to a beautiful little girl two hours later.

Lil' Mark was so proud—this was his second child, and Joy's first. They named the little girl

Marsha, and she was so beautiful.

Joy was full of happiness; her first child... she couldn't wait to be home with her, but the doctor made them stay for a few days for observation before they were released.

Keyshore was named the Godfather, and although he wanted no part in the relationship, he couldn't turn down his place in the baby's life.

LX was salty about the whole situation, though, and Keyshore felt bad for him, but the one thing Keyshore didn't do was let Joy and Lil' Mark's relationship come between the friendship he shared with LX; everyone knew there would be problems in the future from that situation, and it was left like that.

Although Lil' Mark purchased a beautiful house in Sioux Falls, South Dakota for Joy, and the baby, he also bought one in Ellet, too—he had it decked out just for Joy and the baby, and today would be the first day she saw and lived in it.

Joy's mouth dropped when Lil' Mark pulled into the driveway of their Ellet home and told her, "Welcome to our new home."

The house was so beautiful, and Lil' Mark already had everything finished. When she entered the house carrying the baby, tears couldn't stop coming; Lil' Mark was so good to her, and he treated her with so much respect...

Lil' Mark took her for a tour through the house,

showing off every room and the two bathrooms.

***

Zeek raced down Waterloo Road in his new old-school ride. Today was a great day for him; business was going well, and his bitches played their position... what more could he ask for?

He pulled up on his white dude, Keith, to smoke a few blunts, and they sat and smoked blunt after blunt in Keith's driveway.

Keith wasn't your overage white dude, either—he had shit on smash. He also wasn't one of those white dudes that acted black, and Zeek had mad respect for him.

He always had a scam on how to get some money the white-collar way. Today, Keith had a bunch of credit cards that you could max out five thousand on. Zeek laughed hard as he gave him the rundown—Keith showed him all the things he purchased, but Zeek still wasn't interested.

After Zeek got the money Keith owed him, he gave him two more pounds of ice, then left.

Joy having a baby blew his mind, and to find out it was by Lil' Mark was even more surprising. She had just texted him; her and the baby were home safe. She sent her location, and Zeek was headed out to Ellet to them for the first time since she gave birth.

When he got there, Lil' Mark, Keyshore, Brain, Rod, and Roscoe-Cee were all sitting in the living room, smoking blunts, laughing, and talking.

He told Lil' Mark "Congrats," dapped all the homies, then headed into the back room to see Joy and the baby.

He was kind of upset when he got the news that Keyshore was the Godfather, but he settled for being Unc.'

The baby was so beautiful to him as he held her. She was a good baby; she didn't cry very much at all. As he held her, Zeek updated Joy on the business and let her know that all the pounds of ice she'd fronted him were gone, as of today.

Joy hadn't been in the streets since they put the murder game down, and she had no plans to return anytime soon.

Zeek asked, "You want the thirty-K I owe you to be brought over here?"

Joy told him she would get with him in a few days for the money, but Lil' Mark would give him five pounds to hold him off until she got to him.

She shouted for Lil' Mark to come, and he entered the room to see what she wanted. Lil' Mark took care of Zeek, and then Zeek left out on his mission.

Joy cooked wings and fries for the fellas in the meantime—it felt so good to be home in a new house.

By about eleven p.m., everyone was gone, and Lil' Mark went upstairs to find Joy and the baby asleep in the master bedroom. He took off his clothes and climbed in bed with them.

It felt so good to lay next to the woman he loved, with his beautiful child.

The next morning, he was up early changing his daughter's *Pampers* and making a bottle. He couldn't believe how Joy laid asleep while he did everything, but he sang and played with the baby until she went back to sleep.

When Joy finally got up, it was a little after ten a.m. Lil' Mark was all over her kissing and touching her, but she wasn't giving him any pussy, mainly because she still had stitches from the baby.

But he tried and tried until she finally tapped him out with a good blowjob. After he busted a good nut, Lil' Mark laid in the bed in a daze.

Lil' Mark and Joy barely left the house for two months; they spent all their time with the baby. Lil' Mark's other baby mama was caught up in her feelings, so she wasn't letting his daughter with her come over.

But he still went to see the other kid and fuck his other baby's mother; that's just how it was. Joy didn't let it bother her, because she knew he was always coming back home to them.

Joy decided it was time for her to get in the gym—she had to work off that little baby fat. She came and went five times out the week, working harder and harder as the weeks passed.

Lil' Mark saw how dedicated she was, so he built an in-house gym in the basement for them to work out together. He had to give it to Joy; she was a fine art of beauty. Her body was so beautiful, and that ass was so fat.

But with Covid-19 being so bad, Joy didn't go too many places or allow too many people around, and she was always on Lil' Mark about wearing his mask when he was in the streets. Lil' Mark barely went anywhere anyways, but he made sure he stayed masked-up.

He couldn't wait until the shot came to the United States—Covid-19 was fucking up all the legit business, and Covid-19 had the drug prices sky high, so if he and his team weren't so plugged, it would be a hard grind.

Lil' Mark and Keyshore met at a building they co-owned on Brown Street; today was the grand opening.

The building was a very nice size, and inside was the start of three different businesses: they opened a bookstore, a daycare, and a children's clothing store. Although it was a fight with the pandemic still going on, they still went for it.

Lil' Mark allowed Joy the honor of cutting the ribbon, and the small crowd of people affiliated and soon-to-be-employed made their entrance.

Everything was brand new, and the smell of new paint filled the air. Keyshore and Lil' Mark gave each other a firm handshake and smiled—this was the beginning of many more businesses, besides the ones they already started.

Around seven p.m. that evening, Lil' Mark pulled off from the grand opening and headed back to the valley to meet with a few homies who hustled ice for him in the 'hood.

The little Y.B.V.s were up-and-coming, and really starting to make a big name for themselves. These little niggas' ages went from eleven to twenty tops, and they were putting the murder game down like pros.

Since they mostly came up from the bottom of the valley where Lil' Mark and Keyshore grew up, Lil' Mark flooded them with ice, but a lot of tension was in the air with them and the niggas that lived up on the Cheste; the little Y.B.Vs had robbed a few 'hood niggas up the way and refused to give the money back. There wasn't shit anyone could say to convince them otherwise, so Lil' Mark just left the beef amongst them. He gave his opinions, but that was it.

He met Baby-J at Sam's corner store on V. Odom Boulevard.

Baby-J was only thirteen years old, but he looked older. He stood at five-foot and nine inches and weighed a hundred and seventy-five pounds. People tended to think he was older because he already owned his own car, plus, Lil' Mark had him in charge of the ice with his crew.

Baby-J left his car parked and jumped in with Lil' Mark when he pulled up.

"What's the deal, homeboy?" Baby-J shouted as he sat on the passenger side in Lil' Mark's car.

Lil' Mark wasted no time voicing his opinion: he needed Baby-J and his Y.B.V.s to focus more on the ice business than the beefing with everyone.

Baby-J listened, but honestly didn't agree. It was out of respect that he didn't reach in his pants and grab his gun to shoot Lil' Mark.

They rode around smoking blunts of "Za Za," talking about politics around the 'hood, getting money, the future, and the apartment rent Baby-J paid six months at a time.

Lil' Mark's love for Baby-J was strong—the power of a nigga so young was amazing. Baby-J made him thousands of dollars and really moved like he was grown; he even had an eighteen-year-old girlfriend that lived with him.

When Lil' Mark pulled back to the store to drop Baby-J off, he took the gold rope chain with a

Jesus piece off his neck and put it on Baby-J's own neck.

Lil' Mark spoke softly, "Rudimentary, A fundamental element principle or skill. Life is like human chess—so make all your moves premeditated!"

Baby-J nodded his head in agreement, then got out and headed to his car. Lil' Mark pulled off, then headed back home to his baby.

As Baby-J rode, Lil' Mark had left a lot of heavy thoughts on his young mind. Lil' Mark didn't know it, but he had stopped Baby-J from killing a nigga tonight that he'd gotten the drop on. The chain on his neck was shining like he was a rap star, and if he knew the value of it, he would understand why.

Baby-J decided it was best for him to sit in the trap and stay focused on his bag and getting money, so he sent text to all young homies to meet ASAP at the trap; it was time to step the hustle all the way up and slow the beef and robbing. The code was "Murder Bout Money," and that's the way it was going to stay.

***

Joy was up early; she had a doctor's appointment for the baby and herself, and Zeek had some money for her.

She kissed Lil' Mark on the lips, but he was sound asleep and never noticed. Joy got the baby dressed, put her in her car seat, then headed to the doctors.

The baby was healthy and so was she, but the doctor did suggest she give the baby some more fruits and vegetables.

When Zeek met Joy at the grocery store, he jumped in her car, grabbed the bag filled with pounds of ice, and left a book bag of money for her.

After he pulled off, Joy put the bag under the seat, got the baby out, then went into the store.

Joy really enjoyed her new life as a mother and her relationship with Lil' Mark. She knew he cheated, but he made sure there was no disrespect or drama. She still had the hustler in her, but the streets and gang life she seemed to have outgrown.

Although it was Blood life until the death of her, she really wasn't on count anymore, and she knew the first chance they got, they would kill her.

By the time Joy and the baby made it home, Lil' Mark was up, washing clothes and cleaning the house.

Joy smiled at the sight of him being Mr. Super Dad.

She kissed him and told him to grab the groceries from the car, and while Lil' Mark continued with his house duties, Joy decided to cook lunch for them.

***

Baby-J's meeting with the crew went well last night, and everyone was on post getting money. He made sure the whole team was eating, even if he had to take a pay cut.

The tension was still in the air in the 'hood, but for the most part, everyone was focused back on the money.

Baby-J met with Brain at Lanefield to work out, jog, and talk about the beef with the 'up the way' homies. He made it through the workout, but he couldn't hang with all the laps Brain jogged.

He watched as Brain ran lap after lap full of sweat and when Brain finally stopped, they walked laps, just talking.

Brain took a liking to Baby-J quick, and he couldn't believe how young he was. He knew Rod's crew was the problem, and the beef was not with the niggas that ran with him up the way.

The situation was "Murder Bout Money," because Baby-J's crew had robbed a few of Rod's little niggas, which meant money out of Rod's pockets.

Although Rod wasn't tripping—he *did* want the money returned, though—his little niggas weren't allowing a pass.

Brain understood both points of view, but he told Baby-J that Keyshore would be hurt if any more of them killed each other. He also informed him to keep his eyes open, because that beef wouldn't end—even if the money was returned.

It all left Baby-J confused. It seemed like Brain was telling him one thing, but Lil' Mark was stressing something different. He had his crew on chill mode, yet they should stay on guard and ready.

Baby-J drove back to the trap on "The Murder Block," and his crew had the whole street bumping with ice customers. Everyone was strapped even though he told them not to be, and he had to smile at the smartness as he parked and went into the trap with the other homies.

Things weren't adding up.

Baby-J told his crew to remain on guard—the beef was still in the air. Everyone agreed with him, even though they already knew what it was.

Then, he sent Lil' Mark a text and told him he had money for him. Lil' Mark pulled up an hour later with pounds of ice.

Baby-J felt it was best if he didn't mention anything to Lil' Mark about the situation or beef for now.

"I got a few jewels for you Lil' Mark," Baby-J spoke, "Vertical; at right angles to the horizon, a vertical line, plane, circle, etc. Eat or get ate!"

Lil' Mark laughed, then walked out of the trap with the bag of money.

CHAPTER 19

The Beef

Joy jumped on the highway, heading home from the mall. As she was driving, a red Benz that was tinted up drove up on her right side. She looked over but paid it no mind—instead, she looked in the rearview mirror to make sure her daughter was fine.

The baby was drinking her bottle, half asleep, when suddenly shots from the red Benz went off.

Joy was shot in the arm and shoulder, and the baby was shot in the leg. Joy managed to swipe the Benz, making the driver lose control and wreck into a car coming to its left.

She quickly got off on the exit, then wrecked into the back of a car waiting at the light.

Joy was passed out and the baby was crying—blood was everywhere.

The older lady that Joy's car wrecked into got

out to see if she was okay, and when she saw all the blood and bullet holes in Joy's car and heard the baby crying, she dialed 911, then raced to the baby in the car seat in the back.

The baby was shot in the leg, she saw, and by this time, a few other people got out of their cars and rushed to help as well.

The ambulance pulled to the scene five minutes later, and police cars were everywhere. They rushed Joy and the baby to the hospital and listed them in stable conditions.

Lil' Mark was enraged when the call came through—he jumped in his car and rushed straight to the hospital. Keyshore, Rod, Brain, Zeek, Roscoe-Cee, and Baby-J also rushed to the hospital to support their homie and his girl.

Lil' Mark was in tears. Just the thought of his new baby and love of his life both being shot ate away at him.

It seemed like forever until the doctor finally came out and told Lil' Mark the baby was fine; the bullet went in and out and it didn't hit or break a bone. But as far as Joy went, the bullet that hit her in the shoulder was stuck in her back, and the bullets that hit her right arm broke the bone. She would live, but she couldn't go home soon and needed a few surgeries.

They decided they would keep the baby for a few days for observation, and as Lil' Mark spoke with the doctor, Detective V05 and two other officers walked up. They questioned Lil' Mark, but he knew nothing, so they figured they would question Joy when she was able to speak.

Lil' Mark was up all-night drinking and smoking weed. He wanted answers—he wanted to know who shot his girl and daughter. Everyone from his 'hood had their ears to the streets, but so far, nothing came up. All they knew was that it was somebody in a red Benz.

Zeek knew it had to be someone from his Blood gang; he just felt it in his soul. Him and Joy had killed Red Dawg, plus word on the street still stuck that Joy killed Young Ruler.

Zeek was an East side Blood until he died, no matter what the beef was. He remained on the East side, and the Bloods still had love for him—it only the young Bloods that acted funny, but there was nothing they could or *would* do to him.

He drove down Lucy Street, and he pulled up on his homie, Thirst, who was working on one of his houses.

Thirst had like five fiends building a porch and deck in the back yard. He was still shouting and giving orders when Zeek parked and walked up.

Zeek greeted Thirst, then passed him the blunt he was smoking. They talked about the house, and how it was coming along, then Thirst gave

Zeek his condolences and prayers for Joy and her daughter.

Thirst knew where the hit came from, but he wasn't getting involved. He really wished all his Blood homies would let that beef go—too many had already died behind it.

After talking with Thirst for about an hour, Zeek knew he wouldn't get any info out of him, so he left.

***

Baby-J's phone rang, and he pressed ignore. This was the second time his little East side bitch, Kia, had called.

But when the text came by, "*I heard who shot Lil' Mark'S bitch,*" he looked, then dialed Kia's phone.

She picked up on the first ring, and Baby-J wasted no time asking her where she was. When she gave the address on the East side, him and two of his boys headed there immediately.

He thought about calling Lil' Mark, but he thought it would be best if he checked the info out first to see if it was accurate.

Baby-J pulled up on Baird Hill, and Kia and a few other girls were standing on the porch. When she got to the car, he got out to talk with her.

Kia told him how her homegirl—who was on

the porch—told her that Sneeze and Little Snake bragged about riding for Red Dawg in Big Rattle's red Benz.

Baby-J gave Kia two-hundred dollars, a bag of "Za Za," and told her, "Don't mention nothing to anyone else. Make sure your girl don't, either."

She kissed him on the cheek and promised she wouldn't, and Baby-J got back in the car and texted Lil' Mark the names.

Lil' Mark texted back and told him that he was about to text Zeek to see if he knew them.

When Zeek got the text from Lil' Mark, his heart dropped.

The niggas "Sneeze" and "Little Snake" were the fuckboys Red Dawg paid to watch his back in the Summit Lake Apartments. They were there when Zeek and Joy killed Red Dawg.

Zeek told Lil' Mark to meet him on V. Odom Boulevard, ASAP.

Once Zeek ran down the situation to Lil' Mark, everything made sense. Lil' Mark wanted to ride on them right now, but Zeek told him to wait until he got the full drop, and then they could kill them without anyone knowing.

***

Kia called Baby-J at about three o'clock in the morning to let him know that Sneeze and Little Snake were sitting on the porch with her girls, smoking weed. Baby-J thanked her, and realized he had to up her status in his life for her loyalty.

He hung up with her, then texted Lil' Mark. Before he even put his clothes on, Lil' Mark was calling him. Lil' Mark told him to meet him and Zeek on the East side, on Lucy Street.

When Baby-J pulled up on Lucy Street, Lil' Mark and Zeek were standing in front of a grey station wagon, smoking a blunt. He slowed down in front of them, and they both jumped in Baby-J's stolen car.

Baby-J gave them the whole rundown on how they should ambush Sneeze and Snake. He informed them that Kia would call for her friends to come inside when he was ready to attack, to make sure they didn't get involved.

He parked the hot car at the bottom of Baird Hill, and they walked up. Before they got a few blocks away, Baby-J texted Kia, and she texted the green light code back.

Lil' Mark, Zeek, and Baby-J all had their guns out as they snuck up on the house from the side.

Sneeze and Little Snake walked off the porch, heading to the car they had driven to Kia's place.

Lil' Mark was the first to shoot.

He hit Little Snake right in the side of the face, shooting off his ear.

Sneeze was on point, and he fired right back, running then ducking behind the car.

Little Snake started shooting back too, even though his ear was shot off, and Baby-J and Zeek both were shooting, as well—it was a full, bloody shootout early in the morning.

Lil' Mark was pissed. He knew his bad shot cost them a gun battle, but Baby-J ran closer because Little Snake was trying to make it behind the car where Sneeze was shooting from.

Baby-J's bullets struck Little Snake all in the back, and he fell behind the car. Sneeze's bullets hit Baby-J in the chest, knocking him backwards, but Baby-J's bulletproof vest saved his life.

Zeek was right on cue, shooting and covering Baby-J. Lil' Mark reloaded and began shooting again, too. Sneeze looked down, and when he saw that his boy Little Snake was dead, his heart raced with rage—but he knew he was outnumbered.

He crawled into the passenger seat ducked down, started the car, and smashed out.

Lil' Mark shot his whole clip off, but Sneeze got away. Needing to take out his anger, he ran up on Little Snake's lifeless body and kicked him straight in the face.

Baby-J was off to the side, just catching his breath from the bullets knocking the wind out of him.

Zeek shouted, "Let's go y'all!" and they all raced to the stolen car down the street.

Kia's homegirl raced outside after all the shooting stopped, and she fell over Little Snake's body in tears.

The police swarmed from everywhere, and they had to pull her away; they couldn't do anything to save Little Snake—he was dead.

Detective V05 pulled up to the scene thirty minutes later, and he questioned the young ladies at the house Little Snake was killed at. From all the information and evidence, he gathered, it looked like a shootout; Little Snake's gun and its shell casings were found right next to him.

He also learned a guy named "Sneeze" was with him at the time, and he later learned Sneeze's real name was "Jimmy Graham."

"These guys are Bloods," Detective V05 shouted out to the other police officers.

Detective V05 put an APB out on Sneeze; he was wanted for questioning.

Sneeze was in rage; his best friend was dead, and he wanted answers. He made a few calls, and learned the police were looking for him for questioning. He also learned that Lil' Mark may have sent the hit. He was ready for war, and Lil' Mark was a dead man as far as he was concerned.

Baby-J, Lil' Mark and Zeek met up on "The

Murder Block" at Baby-J's trap.

Although Baby-J and Zeek had respect for Lil' Mark, they both felt that he almost cost them their lives.

Baby-J looked Lil' Mark in the eyes and spoke his mind.

He told Lil' Mark, "I understand the anger you felt about your girl and daughter being shot, but next time, it would be best for the ones that get busy a lot to do the shooting first."

Lil' Mark felt offended, and he showed every bit of it.

He told Baby-J, "What you saying? I'm not active, and I can't shoot?"

Baby-J was young, but his heart was big, and he truly felt what he said to Lil' Mark.

They sat and smoked a few blunts, but Zeek never said a word—mainly because he figured he would catch Sneeze on his own time.

Lil' Mark was the first to break the silence.

He informed them that he had to go to the hospital to check on his family, and they all gave him a hug and sent their prayers and blessings for his girl and baby.

After Lil' Mark pulled off, Zeek told Baby-J that he would handle Sneeze, and also that he agreed on what he'd told Lil' Mark.

Baby-J never said a word, but he nodded his head, letting him know he understood.

***

Baby-J stood outside on the Murder Block, selling his ice to his customers. One by one, his niggas formed next him, but he knew they were in the cuts already, watching for his safety; the Y.B.V.s moved like the old Valley Boyz from the 'hood in the 90s.

Kia pulled up on the Murder Block in a dark green truck, and she got out wearing some tight-ass jeans that showed how fat her ass was. At the tender age of seventeen, she was an up-and-coming stallion, and Baby-J was glad to have her on his team; she respected Baby-J's main bitch, Foxy, and played her side bitch position.

"Okay now," Baby-J said as Kia walked up.

Kia smiled and began giving him the rundown; everything was cool, and nobody knew she set the play. The only thing was that her girl told the police Sneeze was with Little Snake.

Baby-J told her, "Don't worry about it, you played it how the police would expect it."

He also let her know that if they didn't give up that info, it would have put red flags up towards them.

Baby-J reached into his pockets and pulled a knot of money out. He counted out two thousand, then gave it to Kia to go shop with and take her girls out.

Kia kissed Baby-J, and before she realized it, she was so happy and in love with him. For him to be so young, he did more than her mother and father put together. The thought of Baby-J being only thirteen years old blew her mind.

***

Lil' Mark sat in the hospital with Joy and the baby. Tomorrow, he would be allowed to take his daughter home.

Joy was scheduled for surgery at the end of the week, but the doctor told her that the bullet sat in a part of her back that wasn't life-threatening. Lil' Mark was happy for all the great news, but Joy's arm was broken and though it already had a cast on it, it still made him upset.

The next day, Lil' Mark brought his daughter in to see Joy and assured her he would hold everything down with her at home.

Four hours later, Lil' Mark and the baby left. Joy was happy, but sad at the same time—she wanted to be home with her family.

Lil' Mark had snuck her some real food in, and she had to laugh at the thought of it again; he looked so guilty when he creP.T. in, looking like Santa on Christmas Day.

He was good to them. He came every day, and

he was the first face she saw when she came out of surgery.

Two weeks later, when the doctor allowed Joy to come home, Lil' Mark was there to get her with the baby.

She hugged them both tight and took in their scent. Joy was glad to be back home and with the most important people of her life.

Once they got back to their place, Lil' Mark did everything because Joy still had a cast on her arm, and Joy felt like the luckiest woman in the world to have him.

***

Zeek couldn't believe his eyes as he drove up towards the house that Thirst worked on—Sneeze was standing right out front, talking to Thirst.

He pulled right up and shot Sneeze before he could reach for his gun.

Thirst clutched his gun, but when he noticed it was Zeek, he backed up.

Zeek shot Sneeze four more times, then drove off, and people in the neighborhood watched in horror as they witnessed him killing Sneeze in broad daylight.

Proudly, Zeek sent Joy a text stating, "Red Dawg's fuckboyz are now all with him!"

Joy smiled and texted back, "Love you, be safe."

She then looked over at Lil' Mark, who was playing with their baby, and said, "Zeek got Sneeze."

He smiled, but deep down inside, he was pissed. He wanted to kill Sneeze himself, but Zeek and Baby-J disregarded his feelings.

Zeek knew Lil' Mark would be upset, but his loyalty was more with Joy than him. He respected him, but it was easy to see Lil' Mark's murder game was washing up.

Zeek hit Baby-J with the news, and Baby-J sent him a salute with respect. Baby-J also told him that Lil' Mark would be mad, but not to sweat it.

Later that night, when Lil' Mark got out of the house, he called Zeek ASAP. He wasted no time telling Zeek how he felt.

Zeek played it cool out of respect for Joy; he told Lil' Mark that he was sorry, but he couldn't take the chance in letting Sneeze get away.

The way he explained it made Lil' Mark feel much better, and Lil' Mark tried to give Zeek ten thousand, but Zeek wouldn't acceP.T. it.

Lil' Mark knew Zeek was like Joy's little brother, so he had to respect that, but he dropped the price on ice for Zeek instead.

Zeek was okay with the lower prices, but when Baby-J got word, he wasn't happy at all because *his* prices didn't change.

***

Brain and Dolf ran smack into each other at Sam's store on V. Odom Boulevard and Ramond Street.

They both clutched for their guns, and people that were around took off in a high-speed walk, knowing some shit was about to go down.

"What's up, motherfucka'?!" Brain shouted at Dolf.

"Whatever you want it to be, bro!" Dolf shouted back.

They both swore on Truck and Wayne G not to shoot each other in the 'hood, but the tension was in the air and the beef was serious—they hadn't run into each other in over ten years.

Dolf was on the run, but he didn't back down.

He told Brain, "You know what it is when we not in the 'hood!"

Brain still shot him in the leg, then jumped in his car and drove off.

Dolf was in pain, but more importantly, he couldn't believe Brain broke the code.

The girl he was riding with rushed him to a

hospital in Canton where his prints came back, and he later was arrested.

When Rod got the news, he was furious, and he called Keyshore with a "911!"

Keyshore met with Rod at the barbershop on V. Odom the next day after Dolf was shot and arrested. Rod told him the whole story that Dolf had told him.

Keyshore couldn't believe it.

He told Rod, "Let me get Brain's side of the story."

Rod informed Keyshore that he already knew that Brain shooting Dolf was about to start a lot of shit.

Lil' Mark pulled up as Keyshore and Rod were talking and smoking a blunt, and they updated him on the whole situation.

All he could do was shake his head.

But Brain must have felt them talking about him, because he also pulled up.

Keyshore asked Brain, "Why did you shoot Dolf?"

Brian said, "Because I wanted to kill him, but I couldn't because I put it on Truck and Wayne G!"

Rod was *pissed,* and before you knew it, he and Brain were in an all-out fist fight. Keyshore let them fight for about two minutes before he and Lil' Mark broke them up.

Keyshore couldn't help but think Brain was losing control as he stormed off and jumped in his car, then pulled off.

Later that night, Brain pulled up and apologized to Rod. He knew he was wrong, but Rod understood their beef was deep and that people had died.

Brain gave Rod eight thousand dollars to put on Dolf's books to feed him, but he also swore Dolf was a dead man if he caught him out the 'hood.

Meanwhile, Dolf sat in the county jail, pissed off, so he had gone and told all his young niggas to shoot Brain on sight.

He couldn't believe Brain shot him, which led him to get locked up for the warrant he had. Dolf cussed out loud to himself—he didn't give a fuck where he saw Brain next; he was shooting him.

Rod got him a top-dollar lawyer and made sure his books was well over good, but when Rod told him that Brain sent him eight thousand, Dolf was even more upset than before.

Rod told Dolf to focus on his current situation and deal with Brain when the time came. Although Dolf was older than Rod, it always seemed like Rod was the little big homie.

***

When Keyshore's house was finally finished, he and Miss Brooks spent their first night in it.

Keyshore had to give it to Miss Brooks; she did her *thang.*

They ate dinner at the new kitchen table by candlelight, and after that, they sat in the living room by the fireplace, viewing the lake through the glass doors.

Love was in the air, and Keyshore was ready to make Miss Brooks his wife.

But as he looked out on the lake, his life flashed before his very eyes. He knew Brain was getting deeper and deeper in the streets, and he refused to let his little brother get killed or land himself back in jail.

Keyshore couldn't stop blaming himself—he was supposed to be out the game before Brian even came home, and yet he wasn't.

Miss Brooks broke his daydreaming when she asked, "What is on your mind? Do you want to talk about it?

Keyshore kissed her and told her, "I love you more than you could ever know."

Miss Brooks was starting to worry about Keyshore, and she let him know exactly how she felt.

CHAPTER 20

When Love Calls Your Name

Keyshore was pushing Christianity, and Brain was pushing Islam. Although they had different beliefs, their insights on life were the same.

Keyshore made it his business to start building with Brain beyond the life in the streets; it was past time for them to conquer their black community and create jobs for the less fortunate.

He couldn't stop thinking about what all the black people went through before their time. Just the thought of how they were out there, killing and doing things to hurt the community the black people before them fought for fucked with his head.

Lately, he started opening up more to Miss Brooks. Although she was an officer, she also was very intellectual—he couldn't believe how much she enjoyed studying black history and how much she knew.

When she taught him about Louis Latimer, it blew his mind. So many black people did important things in America and got little recognition, and he thought it was sad how the black people only got the month of February for Black History Month.

And despite how vicious Brain could be, he was also very semantic and religious. He could talk 'hood shit and switch to politics, spiritual awareness, or culture all in the same breath.

Today was the start of reasoning, and Keyshore made it a day that they would share at least once a week. Brain took over the conversation quick—he talked about what it would take for the unity of street niggas to become strong black men.

He felt that black people who made it legit were too quick to separate themselves from the ones who struggle or choose the wrong path. He used Bill Cosby for instance; he felt that Bill wrote mean things about his black people that cry out for help in this white man's world, but once he experienced the unfair injustice himself, now he understood what the poor, misjudged black men feel every day.

He also explained how in prison, all the Mexicans ate together and moved together; not one Mexican would be left hungry or ate in front of, but the blacks operated in a totally different fashion. When a black inmate was hungry, most of the time, the other blacks wouldn't feed them—why was that?

Brain made sure he had Keyshore full attention before he continued.

"I'll tell you why!" he shouted, "It's because we were taught as slaves to hate each other, cross each other, not trust each other! In order for us to become strong as one, the black people in the higher offices and the wealthy black Americans must truly march together. The big drug dealers must be taught to buy back the community and be backed by the strong, wealthy black Americans—*that's* how you create more jobs for blacks and start a walk for change; we all must move as one, period."

Keyshore had to agree with Brain on a lot of the stuff he spoke about, but he also knew there was more to what he thought himself; the bottom line was that it was time for change and reconstruction.

He was still on getting all his niggas to buy houses or buildings in the 'hood. He figured the more they owned, the closer they were to buying back the 'hood legitimately.

The life they were taught was wrong, and he knew it would take powerful people such as him, Brain, Rod, Lil' Mark, Joy, Baby-J, Roscoe-Cee, and Zeek to change it.

Keyshore tried to get everyone from the team to come to the same reasonings that he and Brain did every week, but one by one, all of them either didn't believe or didn't agree with Keyshore or Brain. Baby-J even laughed in their face; he couldn't believe they spoke the shit they spoke with all the killing and bullshit they had done.

Brain knew Keyshore was hurt at how the team felt, but he also knew the game was always "Murder Bout Money." Nobody but them took the time to think about life after the game and streets. Sad as it was to say, that's exactly how most of the niggas in the game and streets think, until they're dead or their doors lock with long jail sentencings.

***

Kia picked Baby-J up on the Murder Block, and for the last few months he found himself spending a lot of time with her, but if his girl got wind of him with Kia and how he was fucking her, he would never hear the end.

Baby-J was falling hard for Kia and little did he know that Kia had just found out she was a month pregnant by him.

As soon as he got in the truck, he pushed the seat all the way back and started freaking his filter-tip *Mild.* Kia pulled off—today she had to take him to Stow to serve a new customer.

When Baby-J went to light the *Black & Mild,* Kia told him, "I'm pregnant. Do you think you should smoke around me?"

Baby-J damn-near dropped his lighter, he looked over at her with a confused look.

He then repeated her words, "You *pregnant*?"

Kia pulled over to the curve, parked, then looked Baby-J in the eyes and said, "Yes, I'm pregnant—and it's yours, Baby-J!"

Baby-J was lost for words. He didn't know what to say.

Eventually, he rolled the window down and fired up the *Mild.*

Kia continued with the conversation.

She told him that she pissed on the stick, and it read positive. After that, she set up a doctor's appointment—which she just returned from—and they told her that she was six weeks pregnant.

Baby-J wanted a baby, but not this young—or from her. He made sure Kia heard him loud and clear.

"You know I have a girl, and she would kill both of us!"

Kia broke down in tears and screamed, "Fuck your girl! I'm not killing my baby!"

Baby-J couldn't believe his luck with her, and

it was hurting him to see Kia in tears, so he reached over and hugged her, then apologized. He made sure Kia understood that he wasn't out to hurt her, and that he truly liked her.

Together, they came up with a plan and figured it was best to keep the baby a secret.

After Kia took Baby-J to handle all his business, she dropped him back off on the Murder Block. Baby-J kissed her and told her he loved her *and* the baby she was having.

It was the first time ever telling her he loved her, and it brought tears of joy to her eyes and warmed her heart. Gladly, she told him she loved him more.

The moment Kia pulled off, two black chargers with tint pulled up.

Baby-J was caught off guard, with a book bag full of money stamped on his back. He didn't know if it was police or feds, so he didn't clutch for his gun.

The two cars slowed down like they were looking at him, then pulled off slowly.

Baby-J watched as they turned on Eastern Street, and then he walked into the trap to check the cameras.

***

Brain's charm was working wonders as he flirted with his son's teacher.

She had to admit; Brain was everything she desired in a man. After they exchanged phone numbers, he grabbed his son's homework for the week because school was being taught online due to Covid-19.

Before he walked out the door, his son's teacher shouted, "My name is Tamara, by the way!"

Brain pulled his mask off his mouth and said, "I know what your name is."

Tamara smiled, then asked him, "How you know?"

Brain told her, "You teach my son—you don't think I looked you up?"

Tamara busted out laughing.

"He is something else," she thought to herself.

"I'll see you tomorrow for breakfast, Tamara," Brain said as he walked out of the school.

When Tamara got into her car to leave, she noticed a note on her window. She grabbed it, then opened it up—it was from Brain.

He wrote, *"Today, I am thinking of all the reasons I'm so thankful to share this life with you. And I hope you know I have plans of being your partner, lover, best friend, etc."*

Tamara's face glowed with happiness, and she knew there was nothing that would stop her from getting to know Brain.

That next morning, they met for breakfast, and they never left each other's side since. Brain explained his son's mother's situation, and Tamara not only understood, but she also accepted it, too.

He spent the night at her house most the time, but he still went to his baby mother's house as well. With him being Muslim, he was allowed to have more than one wife—as long as he could take care of them.

He worked on Tamara quick, and before you knew it, she was Muslim as well.

***

Joy finally got her cast off today—she was *so* happy to have her other arm back and working again.

Lil' Mark made sure he was with her and the baby everywhere they went, and right now he sat in the waiting room with the baby, waiting for her to come out.

Joy came out with a big smile, threw a few punches at the air happily, then laughed. Lil' Mark got up and hugged her while their daughter tugged at her leg.

The baby wasn't walking yet, but she damn-sure was learning—she was already standing on her own. Joy reached down and scooped her daughter up, kissing her and making her laugh.

Lil' Mark took his family out for dinner that night, and he made sure he was always the best of a gentleman to them.

Joy broke down in tears when he got on his knees and gave her a ring, asking her to be his wife.

She accepted the offer, and people in the restaurant all cheered them on and offered congratulations to both.

***

Keyshore pulled up to the Springhouse, where they sold fresh, beautiful roses and all types of other flowers. He purchased a dozen of red roses for Miss Brooks, and a 'thinking of you' card.

After Lil' Mark told him he was asking Joy to marry him, Keyshore felt it was time he did the same for his own girl.

He already had a two-carat diamond bought for her, and tonight he planned to sweep her off her feet; there was no other woman in the world he wanted to spend his life with.

When he returned home, Miss Brooks was just getting out the shower. Keyshore handed her the dozen roses he had behind his back, and Miss Brooks smiled and shook her head.

"You never cease to amaze me Keyshore," she said as she made her bath towel into a dress around her body and grabbed the roses.

"That's not the only surprise," Keyshore told her as he got down on one knee.

Miss Brooks was in full-on tears in no time.

Keyshore pulled the box with the ring out from his pocket and asked Miss Brooks, "Will you marry me?"

"Yes, yes, yes!" Miss Brooks shouted as Keyshore put the ring on her finger.

Love was in the air and all over their hearts as they made love all through the house.

Keyshore had planned to take Miss Brooks out, but they settled for an at-home date. They walked along the lake in the back of their home, holding hands while the two pit bulls they owned ran around chasing birds.

Miss Brooks told Keyshore how lately, she heard the inmates in jail talk about him, Lil' Mark, Rod, and Brain quite a bit. Keyshore assured her that it came with being successful and out the game—a lot of people thought things they didn't honestly know, so he told her not to worry about it.

***

Business in Canton started to really blossom for Roscoe-Cee—he had the weed on smash. But when he caught his baby mother with a drug dealer from Canton, it broke his heart.

Like always she had told him she had to make a few runs and left the kids home with him. When him and the kids were on the way home from getting a pizza, he pulled in right next to a dude who had his baby mother on the passenger side.

The kids had shouted, "Mommy! Mommy!"

She couldn't hide; she was busted. The light turned green, and Roscoe-Cee didn't even bother to follow them or say a word. He pulled back home and took kids inside. They ate pizza, played family games, then watched a few movies.

Roscoe-Cee baby mother didn't make it in the house until midnight. As soon as she came in, he got all his belongings and had left without saying a word. He figured he would stay in a hotel for a few days until he found an apartment to rent.

His heart was broken, but he handled it like a gentleman.

It took him less than a week to find a two-bedroom apartment. He didn't have much to start with—an airbed, two TVs, a microwave, and a couch—but he continued selling his weed, and little by little, he put his apartment together.

His baby mother only allowed him to see the

kids at her house, which he didn't care about as long as he got to see them.

One night, when he was coming from selling a customer some weed, he ran into a beautiful girl at the gas station named Dorinda. They hit it off good, exchanged numbers, and started going on dates.

Dorinda was such a sweetheart to him, and she had two kids of her own. Roscoe-Cee sometimes felt bad when he took her and her kids out, because his baby mother wouldn't allow him to have his own kids without her supervision.

Dorinda managed to talk Roscoe-Cee into taking the situation with his kids to court, and he later won weekend-visit rights.

***

Detective V05 was starting to put all the pieces together.

He called for a special meeting with the twenty officers he assigned to the "Clean Akron Up" case. He also made a few calls to the FBI—it was time to start applying pressure.

Ever since he made it to lead homicide Detective, the "Clean Akron Up" case officer, Viv, had been very flirtatious with him.

It was such a small world, because Officer Viv and Deputy Sheriff Miss Brooks happened to be close friends. Viv had been driving Miss Brooks nuts about how she liked Detective V05, and Miss Brooks urged her to push up on him or do something to let him know she wanted to know him outside of work.

So today, Viv gave it a shot.

She walked into the meeting room before everyone came and asked Detective V05 straight up, "Would you like to go on a date?"

The question caught V05 off guard, but he was very attracted to Viv and wouldn't pass up the offer.

He smiled, then told her, "I would love to take you on a date."

After Detective V05 finished his meeting with the police officers, he updated them on how they might also be bringing in ten deputy sheriffs as well. Everyone had personal folders when they left and understood how important the information was.

Viv made sure she was the last to leave, and V05 couldn't help but admire her beauty and shape as she did.

When Viv got in her car, she quickly called Miss Brooks with the news about her going on a date with V05.

Miss Brooks was all smiles as her girl went on and on about how V05 made her feel. He was mixed with black and white, he stood six-foot one, two-hundred and fifteen pounds of muscle, with the most beautiful eyes she had ever seen.

Detective V05 chose to take Viv on a date she would always remember.

First, he took her to the Cleveland Museum of Art. Viv was amazed how much Detective V05 knew about the business and quality of art. They walked hand-in-hand as he showed her all the extravagance in art.

After they left the art museum, he took her to play laser tag, which was very fun and a lot of exercise.

Viv was truly having the time of her life.

The night ended with a very fancy and expensive restaurant that sat on the Lake Erie. They sipped fine wine and ate the best seafood ever.

Viv didn't make it home until close to eleven o'clock that night. Detective V05 opened the car door for her and walked her to her doorstep.

He kissed her hand and told her, "I hope we can go on many more dates."

Viv accepted the offer and thanked him for being a gentleman and showing her a great time.

When she got inside her house, she wasted no time calling Miss Brooks with the scoop on her date.

They laughed and talked all the way until Viv

got a text from Detective V05, letting her know he was home safe. Viv hung up with Miss Brooks and texted V05 back and forth until they called it a night.

From then on, they continued to date and see each other.

CHAPTER 21

The Ominous

Skelton had shit on smash in the best way; his monopoly was growing at a fast rate, and he wasted no time putting down the murder game and buying all the property he could.

Mandan, North Dakota was his city, and 2nd Avenue was his block—you couldn't tell him anything different. He had a team of hungry young niggas that were getting money and killing shit every time he sent them.

Skelton pulled up on 2nd Avenue to the trap, and as soon as he parked, two of his young Boyz were on guard, ready to die or kill for him.

He got out wearing a big, gold rope chain with a 2nd Avenue charm on it, a bust-down Rolex watch, and a diamond earring in one of his ears. He was dressed in a Gucci t-shirt, Gucci jeans, and Gucci shoes, and you could see the butt of his "FN" pistol on his hip. When he smiled at the sight of his little niggas, his mouth was full of solid gold teeth.

They all entered the bottom apartment of the two-complex house. Inside was enough guns laying around to go to war with, and the whole house was flooded with cameras from outside to the inside.

Two more young dudes appeared as they entered the front room, and in the back, four more young dudes were smoking weed, playing video games, and talking shit.

Skelton sat in the living room and signaled for everyone to join him.

"Tonight," he spoke very low and clear, "We murder all new competition and rob them for all their goods. They will respect 2nd Avenue, *and* our movement—period!"

All eight of his young Boyz shouted out, "Murder Bout Money!"

Skelton smoked a few blunts with his young Boyz, then went up to the upstairs apartment to count the money they made.

Business was good, but his greed and power were starting to overtake him—he couldn't even keep a steady chick for the same reasons, but he didn't care.

Later that night, Mandan, North Dakota turned into a killing ground. Skelton and his young Boyz moved like the mob, killing, and robbing as they went.

The last dude they hit's name was "Florida," because that was where he was from. Florida had 1st Avenue on smash with a team of young Boyz, as well.

Skelton and his crew decided to raid on foot, which was their biggest mistake.

As they creP.T. up from behind two houses, Florida and his team were mingling, sitting, and standing on the porch.

Shots rang out, but Florida was quick on his toes as he rolled off the porch, shooting two of Skelton's young Boyz in the chest and head. Then he jumped back up, shooting as he backstepped towards a van on the curve.

Skelton responded by shooting his right-hand man in the back before he could make it off the porch, and seeing his little nigga fall from a bullet in the back drove Florida crazy.

He stepped out from behind the van, shooting two more of Skelton's young Boyz in retaliation.

Finally, Skelton signaled for his team to retreat; two of his Boyz were dead, and two were shot, so they raced back behind the house to the cars that were waiting.

When Florida stepped back up to his trap, he looked at the dead bodies of four of his Boyz, one being his right-hand man, Lil' Akon. Anger filled his heart, and he kicked the dead bodies of Skelton's own two young Boyz.

Police sirens were nearing, so Florida and the rest of his team raced down the street to his safe house.

Skelton and *his* young Boyz made it back to the trap on 2nd Avenue, but his two little niggas that got shot in the leg and arm had to go to the hospital the next county over.

Mandan, North Dakota was up in an uproar as news stations flashed the six dead bodies of the young teenage kids involved in what seemed to be a drug and gang war.

News traveled fast, and Marshall was texting Skelton and asking him what the fuck he had going on. Skelton knew he fucked up and knew he didn't think things out correctly. He was the cause of the murder rate going up, but little did he know it only made him hot.

When it rains, it pours. That next week, the feds hit hard; they grabbed ten of Skelton's young Boyz and caught him upstairs in the trap with close to a million dollars in cash.

He was named the head of a twenty-five-man indictment conspiracy—not to mention the outstanding triple homicide warrant he had from Akron, Ohio.

"Skelton," aka Sam Johnson's name was

blasted all over every news station in North Dakota. He even made Goldie hot, because they now were showing mugshots of him, too, and giving his name: Chris Gibson, aka "Goldie."

When Marshall called him and told him to check out the news, he couldn't believe it—Chris Gibson, aka "Goldie" was wanted in connection to a triple homicide in Akron, Ohio.

Although Goldie had picked up about fifty pounds, he still looked about the same, but the fact that he still used his street name really gave him away.

It was time to get out of North Dakota, and fast. Brain made arrangements for him to flee to the ATL, and he was gone in the blink of an eye.

Lil' Mark got the news, and he made sure Marshall shut everything down. Things were getting hot by the second, and no one could believe how Skelton crashed the million-dollar business like that.

Keyshore and Lil' Mark were scared to death; they didn't know what to think or do. They changed numbers constantly, but they also lost a half of a million with Skelton going to jail.

Marshall never stood a chance as he sat behind the counter of his restaurant.

Feds rushed in. They raided all his restaurants, his home, condo, beach-house in Florida, and his other establishments. They found nothing—no drugs or money—but they still took him because they found him through Skelton's phone being wired.

Although they had nothing to give Marshall a long time, they had enough to see if they could get him to tell them something.

When he got to the federal holding spot in North Dakota, they moved him onto the same pod as Skelton and a few of his young Boyz.

Marshall was beyond pissed—he couldn't believe Skelton called him using a hot-ass phone when he was supposed to only use his trap phone.

Skelton sensed the anger in Marshall's face when they locked eyes, but he still walked up and gave some love.

He showed Marshall his paperwork and told him that the feds only had them having one conversation. He also told Marshall that it wasn't about drugs, it was about money, so the feds couldn't use any of the cars from him since Skelton owned a car dealership.

Just hearing that eased Marshall's mind a lot, and the fact that they didn't take any cars, properties, or bank accounts only made it better.

He was stuck, though, and the feds wanted him to tell—*bad.*

Skelton wasted no time taking over the federal holding spots. He got a guard to start bringing tobacco, weed, cellphones, and K2. Skelton was right back to handling business from the fence, but Marshall wanted no part. He didn't even want a free cellphone; he decided the payphone was best for him.

Skelton ended up meeting a Mexican and convinced him to front him fifty pounds of ice right from jail. Skelton still had people that would move for him all through North Dakota, and just like that, he was back to getting money from on the streets to inside the jail walls.

Goldie stayed in the ATL for a few months but couldn't adjust to it, so he headed right back to Akron under the feds' noses. Roscoe-Cee convinced him to hide out in Canton, but Brain told him it wasn't safe because the feds were on Roscoe-Cee, too, so Keyshore ended up getting Goldie a safe spot out in Stow.

Goldie played the house, and his friends made sure all his needs got met. He also turned Skelton up to his people in North Dakota, although he couldn't believe how Skelton managed to find a plug-in jail, or how he had a cellphone.

Brain didn't like Goldie talking to Skelton. They all knew *he* was doing the most, but he let Goldie do what he wanted. Crazy as Skelton was, he managed to pay Keyshore, and Lil' Mark back the money he owed from right where he was at in jail.

But still, nobody gave him any more drugs—except the Mexican.

***

Baby-J stepped out from behind the trap on the Murder Block and shot his little nigga, Alex, right in the side of the head.

Blood gushed out his head as it exploded from the other side.

"Bitch, you want to steal from the gang?!" he shouted, with spit flying out of his mouth.

Alex's eyes laid lifelessly open as Baby-J kicked him in the face, then went into his pocket, taking his money and the gun off his hip.

Things were getting bad for Baby-J. He was taking loss after loss.

Just the day before, he found out Alex was stealing; he wrecked his car running from the police, and he left a pound and a half behind when he jumped out and ran.

As much as he had promised Lil' Mark he wouldn't rob, the temP.T.ation was back. He was down ten thousand of the money he owed Lil' Mark, and if he paid him out, his stash he would be broke.

Too much laying up fucking, partying, and

shopping had caught up with him. And now he didn't even have his car, which only made matters worse.

***

Joy thought she saw a shadow run past the window as she was washing dishes, so she quickly ran into the living room and grabbed the gun hidden on top of the cabinet.

"Where the fuck is Lil' Mark?!" she thought as she made sure the baby was okay, still sleeping.

Boom! Boom! Boom!

Her back door flew open, and three masked men ran in, guns in hand. Thankfully, they couldn't have seen Joy, who was now hiding right by the door to the kitchen.

When she peeked in, she saw two dudes ransacking the kitchen cabinets, looking for something.

She wasted no time firing her gun until the clip was empty.

Two of the three men ran out, but they had all been shot, and one masked man laid dead on her kitchen floor.

Joy was in tears as she called Lil' Mark.

When she pulled the mask off the intruder's face, her heart dropped.

He was a kid.

The little boy couldn't have been older than fourteen or fifteen years old...

By the time Lil' Mark made it home, his house was full of police, homicide detective V05, and the crime unit.

The little boy's body was still lifeless in his kitchen, and when he got a good peek at it, he knew it was Baby-J's Y.B.V nigga, "Jonge."

Anger filled his heart, but he had to remain cool.

Detective V05 was really starting to worry about Joy as he questioned her.

He asked her why someone would be after her, and he also wondered why they had been searching her kitchen. Did she have drugs or something?

Something was strange about this situation, but Joy had a clean record, so he couldn't do much but watch her and her friend closer.

The dead man's name came back as "Jonge Frenchman." He was in the gang file known to be a Y.B.V; a younger street gang from the Valley. He was only fifteen years old, but he had already been to D.Y.S twice for robbery.

Just a few days ago, another kid named "Alex Maze" was found dead with a shot to the head on the Murder Block.

"What a coincidence," Detective V05 thought to himself, *"Two Y.B.V kids dead in two days…"*

The next day, Lil' Mark was blowing Baby-J's phone up at seven o'clock in the morning. After about his third time calling, Baby-J answered half asleep.

Lil' Mark was shouting so loud that Kia—who was in bed with him—could hear him, so Baby-J got up and went to the bathroom.

"Calm down, bro!" Baby-J shouted, before asking him to explain what he was talking about.

Lil' Mark told him that Jonge and two of his other dudes tried to rob his house last night.

"Jonge is dead, too—Joy killed him!" he shouted over the phone.

Baby-J went silent.

Jonge was one of his top niggas, and he couldn't believe he was dead… or even the fact that they had been robbing Lil' Mark's house.

When he got it together, Baby-J told Lil' Mark to let him see what was going on, because he honestly had no idea.

Lil' Mark didn't trust Baby-J's word, but he decided to play it cool until he figured shit out. Instead, he quickly got Keyshore on the line, and Keyshore was full of rage.

Keyshore then told Brain and Rod about the situation, and from there, a war in the 'hood started quickly.

Baby-J knew it was coming, but he couldn't believe Jonge got so thirsty that he went on that mission.

Word got back quick about the other two dudes Joy shot that were with Jonge, and by the end of the week, word spread that Brain and Rod killed them right in front of Sam's store on V. Odom Boulevard.

The green light wasn't on Baby-J, but he was still wanted by Keyshore and Lil' Mark. Niggas in his crew were getting shot left and right—they couldn't even hustle in the 'hood.

Baby-J made Kia put tint on her windows. She was pregnant, and a war was coming Baby-J's way fast, it seemed.

He decided it was best for them to lay low in the Joy Park apartments over at his cousin's house, but Baby-J kept his AR, thirty-clip 40-cal, and bulletproof vest on him. He wasn't taking any chances, and he damn-sure wasn't about to die before he turned fourteen years old next month. Not to mention, Kia was already close to seven months, and they found out months ago that they were having a little boy.

Lil' Mark and Brain had been calling him daily, but he refused to meet up with them. Brain gave his word that they wouldn't kill him, but he had heard too many stories about Brain to trust his word.

***

Skelton had Jada living lavishly—she couldn't believe the power he had from jail. He bought her a 2022 Jaguar XJS convertible that black on black, and she shopped at all the best fashion stores; from Neiman Marcus and Saks, to Nordstrom and Bloomingdale's.

And she *also* controlled the streets of North Dakota. The Mexicans came to her with the product every time, and she exchanged the money. Jada was in a sexual relationship with the federal C.O lady that Skelton dealt with, too.

Skelton had a lot of gangster shit going on, and he made sure both women got the best care. Being Muslim was working in his favor, too; it allowed him to have as many wives as he could afford.

Brain had brought him into Islam when he was about ten years old, so his knowledge and wisdom was very strong by now.

And although the cases he had weren't looking good, his pockets sure were. He figured that if he never got out, he could at least invest back into his 'hood with Keyshore and Brain, so Skelton wasted no time buying houses in the 'hood like

Keyshore always wanted them to.

CHAPTER 22

Covid-19 Meds Not Working

Miss Brooks wasn't feeling good, but she still got up and got dressed for work.

The inmates in Summit County Jail had been on lockdown for months due to the Covid-19 outbreak, but she always wore her mask and kept her hands clean.

Keyshore was still asleep when she left out the door for work.

Everybody that worked in the county jail took temperature checks before they were allowed into the jail, and when Miss Brooks took her check, her temperature was over a hundred, which wasn't good at all. They took it again just to be certain, but it was still the same, so she was sent home until she got tested.

Later that night, she still wasn't feeling well, so she went to the hospital, where she tested positive for Covid-19.

Keyshore couldn't believe it. They tested him too, but strangely, he didn't have it—at least, not yet. He still had to quarantine for two weeks to be safe, though.

After his two weeks of quarantining, Miss Brooks' condition had worsened, and she was placed on a ventilator.

Keyshore felt like his whole life crumbling in front of him. He couldn't think or sleep knowing that Miss Brooks was hooked to all those machines, fighting for her life.

The doctor informed him that things weren't looking good for her, and gently advised him not to count on her to pull through.

Keyshore hit the floor in tears when he received the news.

"It has to be a dream," was all he kept telling himself, but it wasn't.

A week later, Miss Brooks passed away from Covid-19. She died at the age of thirty-seven years old, with no children, and she died with the ring on her finger that Keyshore had bought when he asked her to marry him.

Although Viv didn't really know Keyshore, she knew how much Miss Brooks loved him. It crushed her heart, and she also felt Keyshore's pain.

But Keyshore wasn't himself without Miss

Brooks, and he was really turning into an alcoholic. He stayed in the house for weeks, drinking himself to sleep and crying.

***

Zeek pulled up on Baby-J in the Joy Park apartments. Baby-J trusted Zeek for some reason, and since Zeek felt that Baby-J didn't set Joy up to get robbed, he was the only person he could re-up with since he didn't trust the rest of the team anymore.

He was in Zeek's hood on the East side, and business started picking up, so Baby-J spent his last bit of money with Zeek, which was close to thirteen thousand. Zeek fronted him everything he bought, and gave him a pound of weed to sell, too.

Baby-J was also a father now; Kia had had their son the day after he turned fourteen years old, so as a man, he felt that he had to take care of his new family—even though he was still a kid himself.

Brain watched as Zeek came out of the apartment Baby-J was in.

He had been watching Baby-J for almost two weeks now, and it threw him for a loop to see Zeek doing business with him.

Zeek got into his rental car, then pulled off, and Brain stood beside the dumpster for a few more hours before he called it a night.

He had noticed Baby-J had a nice flow of traffic coming in and out the apartment. He also noticed that Baby-J had a newborn baby, and a very young girl was hanging around him who must have been the mom. Another thing he noticed that the older woman who the apartment belonged to resembled Baby-J a lot—maybe a relative.

Brain was hungry, and not the type of hungry that you wanted after you. Although he believed Baby-J had no part in the situation with Joy and Lil' Mark's house, the fact that he'd kept refusing to meet angered him.

He walked out of the Joy Park apartments to his car that was parked on Morton Avenue, then pulled off to take care of a few other things.

***

The Covid-19 vaccine finally landed in the United States, but for some reason, the meds weren't kept at the temperature that they were supposed to be.

With that being said, a lot of people became sick from the shots, or they simply weren't working, and the infection rates of the Covid-19 outbreak was continuing to rise.

Although the curfew time was lifted in Ohio, people were still required to wear masks in public. A lot of people ended up catching fines because they weren't following those guidelines.

Keyshore had a small ceremony for Miss Brooks. Although her family had her cremated a month ago, he felt it was only right for the people that were around him that loved her too to get the chance to mourn and remember the good things about her.

The whole crew showed up at the hall he rented on Grant Street. Keyshore's older cousin was a pastor, so he led the ceremony.

All eyes dropped when Baby-J stepped in, holding his son with Kia on his arm.

Lil' Mark damn-near jumped out of his seat, but Joy grabbed him and stopped him. Baby-J sat in the back row, as the ceremony was already in process, and he didn't want to disturb it.

Roscoe-Cee even showed up with his new girlfriend—it shocked everyone to see him without his baby's mother.

Everyone laughed and cried as they remembered the great times with Miss Brooks. Her best friend did the ending prayer and gave blessings to the wonderful food they ate afterwards.

After Baby-J finished his plate, he gave his son

to his mother, and he and Lil' Mark went to the back room to talk.

They talked for close to an hour, and as mad as Lil' Mark was, his love for Baby-J was strong. He had practically raised Baby-J and looked at him as a son. Deep in his heart, he knew Baby-J wouldn't have ever done such a thing as rob him.

Baby-J apologized to everyone in the crew one by one, and he admitted that he was afraid.

He hugged Keyshore tight and gave him his condolences about Miss Brooks. He told him that Keyshore losing Miss Brooks was what made him finally face the team.

Keyshore held him tight and spoke in his ear.

"Never fear the family. Even if you are wrong, acceP.T. your responsibility."

Brain also let him know that he knew exactly where Baby-J was, and he had seen Zeek at his spot. Zeek was in shock, but he had to laugh—he loved Brain's style. Brain was truly a warrior.

Zeek was all over Viv during the gathering, and when Keyshore told him she was a police officer, that only turned him on more. They danced and talked the night away.

Although Viv was dating Detective V05, it wasn't that serious, and they never made any stipulations. As far as she was concerned, she was single and able to mingle.

The wine was talking to her, and so was Zeek

with his good game.

When Keyshore spotted them headed to the door to leave together, he shook his head with a grin.

Zeek followed Viv to drop her car off at her house, and then she got in with him. He decided to take her to his apartment since she seemed a *little* too tipsy for anything else, but he laughed at how she continued to remind him that she was a police officer.

When they got to his place, she was amazed at how nice and neat he kept it.

Zeek put on some slow music and gave her a hand to join him in a slow dance. Viv accepted his offer, and then they danced to a few songs.

But Viv couldn't control herself—she wanted Zeek. The bad-boy swag he had turned her on a lot.

She kissed him softly on the lips, then harder as their tongues danced with one another. Before they knew it, clothes were falling off everywhere, and they had some great, hot sex.

Viv woke up the next morning, naked in Zeek's arm. She couldn't believe she had a one-nightstand with him, but she also wasn't about to miss some morning sex, either.

She woke him up with her mouth sucking and kissing his dick. When she noticed he was awake, she told him a quick “good morning,” and continued sucking his dick.

Zeek’s toes began to curl up—Viv was putting it on him *good.*

As he moaned, “Oh my god,” Zeek pulled his dick out from her mouth and told her it was time he took control of this situation.

He took his time making love to Viv and made her experience feelings she hadn’t felt in a long time. Viv came at least four times that morning, and she had to thank Zeek—he was *that* good.

When they were all finished, Zeek cooked her a nice breakfast. He made her eggs, toast, bacon, and cheese grits with fresh-cut fruits. His charm was really on as he fed her pieces of fruits once she finished her plate.

Viv was very impressed, and Zeek made it be known that he wanted to see her again and hopefully make something special of it.

They talked and found that they had a lot of the same life views, and Viv really felt a lot of great energy from Zeek in general.

The big question was about the differences in their lives. Although Zeek kept his drug life a secret, Viv was heavily involved in her job. She worked a lot of long hours, and her life was always in danger when she worked the cold streets of Akron.

Zeek let her know that he understood

everything, and he also let her know that it was okay for them to take their time.

After Zeek dropped Viv off at home, her mind couldn't stop thinking about him. He really made her feel so good, and she felt so close to him so soon...

She shook her head as she got into the shower—she knew she had a lot of thinking to do.

***

Detective V05 and his raid team geared up to invade a home that an anonymous tip was given regarding Chris Gibson, aka "Goldie."

This was his first big sting since he been named Lead Detective to the police force and "Clean Akron Up." His nerves gave him the shakes a little, but he figured it was just the rush and too much coffee-drinking.

The team had been watching the apartment Goldie stayed in for a week now. When the lady informant that gave his name up told officers about the situation, she explained how her and two of her girls did sex acts for money. She had noticed his face on the Most Wanted list, and she couldn't pass up the reward money.

Six o'clock that morning, Detective V05 and the "Clean Akron Up" raid team burst into the apartment.

The sound of them knocking the door down made Goldie grab the AR that laid next to him. All he saw was people in black, and he rolled out of his bed and onto the floor.

Before he could hear them say, “Police; search warrant,” he was already letting off shots from his gun.

The first two officers that entered the room got shot multiple times, and if it wasn’t for the bulletproof vest and riot gear, their lives wouldn’t have existed anymore.

Gunfire went off for three minutes straight.

Goldie was shot too, but his own bulletproof vest saved *his* life, as well.

After the house was cleared, V05 found multiple guns, and close to fifty-thousand in cash.

Goldie was taken to the hospital for gunshot wounds but nothing life-threatening. He was now charged with multiple attempted assaults on a police officer, a few gun charges, plus the triple homicide.

Goldie made the news all over the world, and Skelton felt sick when word got to him. He made sure he got rid of the phone he and Goldie talked on, but he made sure ten thousand got put on Goldie’s books and put twenty-thousand towards his lawyer.

Brain's heart was hurt as he and Keyshore watched the news for the third time, but there wasn't shit they could do; Goldie was going to jail for a long time. Their only hope was for him to beat the murder charges, at least.

Detective V05 came on Channel 19 News and informed the city of Akron, Ohio that he was the new man on the job, and his "Clean Akron Up" raid team would do just that.

Zeek's face turned up at what he heard Detective V05 saying on the T.V.

When Goldie made it to Summit County jail, all his 'hood dudes seemed to be in there fighting big cases. He didn't feel so bad about being all over the news, though, since his homeboy Joe Fletch was "public enemy number one," as well.

Goldie knew he was in deep trouble, but he didn't allow it to bother him. His team made sure his books were straight and lawyer was paid—what more could he ask for?

When Homicide Detective V05 came to interview him, he did what every nigga in the streets should; he walked in, sat down, and when Detective V05 asked him what happened, he asked for his lawyer and shouted for the guards to take him back.

Detective V05 was so upset, he wanted to

choke all the life out of Goldie. When the guards finally came, Goldie blew Detective V05 a kiss, and told him have a blessed day.

***

Baby-J was back on Murder Block, holding the drug game down. He did a lot of things different now; nobody in the gang was allowed to rob, and he made sure everyone had a bag or a job that paid them. Just for that good behavior, Lil' Mark upped his supplies.

Joy sat on the porch at the trap, just to let her presence be known. She felt that if any of the gang had a problem with her, then she was going to deal with them herself.

Baby-J had to laugh when he looked up and noticed how serious Joy was looking. Joy was a beautiful woman, he had to admit, but a cold-blooded killer, as well.

Joy shouted for Baby-J to send someone to grab some blunts, so Baby-J reached in his pockets and gave his runner twenty dollars to get some blunts and water bottles.

He then walked up on the porch and asked Joy, "You smoking with me?"

The two of them talked until his runner returned with the blunts, then Joy had Baby-J roll up five blunts.

Joy decided to get all the young niggas high, so she told Baby-J to call the other five niggas from the gang on the porch, and they chain-smoked blunt after blunt of the "Za Za" weed.

She had to admit; she liked the young niggas. She couldn't believe how young they were, but they were up on the game. The oldest one was Baby-J, and he was only fourteen years old. All five of them kept a gun on them, too—it just really blew her mind.

Everybody from the gang told Joy they had no hard feelings towards her; they understood the game. They let her know that they would have done her people the same way, under the same circumstances.

Joy was high and lost in a daze, but she missed her 'hood on the East side. The fact that her Blood gang wouldn't acceP.T. her back hurt her. She had put in so much work for her 'hood growing up and was *so* loyal to LX and the Blood gang...

Eventually, Joy got up, gave all the little niggas a handshake, then pulled off.

CHAPTER 23

Falaz Expresión, Fideicomiso Opcional!

Rod smacked the gun out the young dude's hand who had it pointed at him. He quickly reached to his hip and upped his own gun, shooting the young dude right in the chest.

He couldn't believe the young nigga tried him in the parking lot of the "Clutch" strip club.

Rod jumped back in his truck and pulled off, mad at the whole situation. He quickly called Keyshore as he jumped on the highway. Keyshore picked up on the second ring, and Rod wasted no time telling him that he just shot a nigga at the bar. Keyshore couldn't believe what he was hearing—he told Rod to meet him in the 'hood.

Keyshore was parked in the driveway that connected to the barbershop on V. Odom when Rod pulled up.

Rod jumped in, and Keyshore took him to get rid of the gun and switch clothes because it was a must to set the ones he'd worn on fire.

On the way back from Cleveland, Rod told Keyshore he was getting out of town for a while. He felt a lot of heat coming on in Akron, and he had too much to lose to start fucking around. He figured he would go lay up in Texas for a while with his Mexican girl, since she's been on his ass for ages about never visiting her there.

Keyshore agreed with him on taking a vacation; he wouldn't miss any money with the way Brain started running through the coke.

The sun was coming up by the time Keyshore dropped Rod back off to his car, and he had writing in lipstick all over his truck from what seemed like one of his upset female friends.

Keyshore laughed and shook his head as Rod poured water from a bottled water on an old shirt to clean off the writing.

***

"2022 is becoming a bad year already," Rod thought as he got on the airplane heading to Houston, Texas.

His Mexican woman, Sinfonia couldn't wait for him to come. She had been bragging to all her friends for years about Rod, and as soon as he landed and got off the plane, Sinfonia was right there waiting for him.

He had to admit; she truly was a beautiful woman that knew how to treat her man.

Rod hugged and kissed Sinfonia the moment he walked up on her.

"You look really nice," he told her as they headed to grab his luggage.

Rod figured he wouldn't pack too much, so he only had a few bags.

Sinfonia had the whole day planned for them, but she took him to her condo first to freshen up.

As soon as they entered her condo, Rod was all over her. He picked her up and sat her on the kitchen counter and slowly pulled her shorts off, then her panties.

Sinfonia moaned with pleasure as Rod kissed her leg and licked her inner thighs. She wanted him to taste her clean-shaved pussy so bad, but he continued to tease her.

He sucked and licked all over her breast, then he worked his way back down, and this time, he stuck his fat wet tongue directly in her pussy.

Sinfonia's eyes rolled back into her head as Rod tongue-licked the rim of her asshole, and then glided back to her clit.

She grabbed his head and started to fuck his face as his tongue danced all around her clit.

When Sinfonia couldn't take it anymore, her

body began to shake as she grinded harder up against Rod's face and tongue.

"Awwwwww!" she screamed as she climaxed all over Rod's face.

Rod kissed her right in the mouth so she could taste her sweet-tasting pussy, and she sucked on his tongue as he entered her with his solid, hard dick.

His strokes started off long, and then short as she moaned with acceP.T.ance.

Sinfonia couldn't stop cumming. Rod was right on a spot and stroking it just perfect, getting her to cum over and over and over.

Right before he climaxed, he pulled his dick out and Sinfonia got on her knees and sucked it until he came all in her mouth.

***

Joy woke up after the fifth night in a row that Lil' Mark didn't come home at night. She washed the baby up, dressed her, then made breakfast.

Lil' Mark finally came in at nine o'clock that morning while her and the baby watched cartoons. When he went to kiss Joy, she smacked his face away, so he picked his daughter up and started playing with her.

Joy was in rage as she shouted, "I don't know what type of bitch you trying to play me for!"

Lil' Mark couldn't believe she was speaking in such language towards him.

He sat the baby down and explained to Joy, for what seemed like the thousand time, that he had another daughter and just because he and his other daughter's mother didn't see eye to eye, he couldn't dishonor his other daughter.

Lil' Mark was in process of getting his custody rights with the courts, but for the time being, his other daughter wanted him home with her some nights.

Joy didn't give a fuck about what he was talking about.

"If you miss one more night not coming home, then don't *ever* come back."

Lil' Mark sensed the hurt in Joy's voice. Even though he honestly wasn't having sex with his other baby's mother anymore since he asked Joy to be his wife, he knew it was wrong.

"It won't happen again, Joy," he apologized, and accepted being in the doghouse for a few days.

But he worked his way right out of the doghouse again; he cooked, cleaned, took his family on dates...

Joy couldn't resist her love for Lil' Mark. He was everything she could ask for, and she prayed the custody situation with the courts ended quickly.

The next month, the courts granted Lil' Mark weekends only with his daughter, so she was allowed to stay with him from Friday until Sunday morning.

It felt good for Lil' Mark to finally be able to spend time with both his daughters at the same time. Although they were three years apart, he really wanted them to know and love each other.

***

The gambling spot on the Murder Block was packed with gamblers and beautiful women, but Keyshore was sweating, as he had a five-hundred-dollar bet on the dice.

His point was four, and he also had three ten-to-four bets for a hundred each. Zeek was fading him, and Roscoe-Cee had a hundred-dollar bet along with Baby-J and Thirst.

Keyshore hit the ten two times in a row, picking up six hundred dollars, so Brain decided to bet with Keyshore. In turn, Zeek bet two hundred on the straight and a hundred on the ten-to-four.

He hit the ten two more times, and he and Brain picked their money up each time, talking shit.

After about five more rolls, Keyshore hit the four and grabbed all the money he won. But when

Brain went to grab *his* money, Zeek put his foot on one of the hundred-dollar bills, stating that he didn't bet back on the ten-to-four bets.

Before Brain knew it, he swung and hit Zeek right in the face, sending him to the floor. Brain grabbed the hundred-dollar bill Zeek's foot was on, then put it in his pocket.

Zeek got up and pulled his gun out, but everybody was strapped and pulled theirs too.

Brain was furious, and he shouted, "Oh, you want to pull yo' gun cause you tried to cheat me, and I punched your bitch-ass?!"

Keyshore quickly stepped in between the situation. He knew Zeek had little chance because he wasn't from the 'hood, but at the same time, he was family.

"Listen Zeek," Keyshore said, "you never offed the bet. And Brain, you're wrong for punching him; we're all family."

Baby-J went in the back room, then came back holding two sets of boxing gloves.

"Why don't y'all old niggas settle it the old-school way? My money's on Zeek!" Baby-J shouted.

Everybody began making bets, so Zeek and Brain took it outside to the parking lot with the gloves.

It turned out to be a great fight—they went five rounds. Brain lost, but only because he ran out of gas and didn't want to go to the six rounds.

After the match, they dapped and kept the love and respect towards each other. Keyshore was proud of how they handled it, so he made the party on him by paying for all the drinks and weed.

***

Sinfonia pulled up to her uncle's house so he and Rod could meet each other, because they had only met on Facetime prior. Her uncle had a nice, big ranch, and Rod was amazed by all the animals and land.

"What's up tío?" Sinfonia called as he greeted them at the front door.

Tío hugged Sinfonia and she continued her way inside, while he and Rod took a walk through the ranch.

Tío informed Rod that he had a nephew in Dayton, Ohio that he wanted him to meet in the future. His name was Black Jefe, and he promised Rod that they would like each other.

Tío continued giving Rod all the knowledge he needed to know about Texas and the Mexicans, since Rod planned to stay for a while.

He was also impressed at how Rod ran through the bricks of coke the way he did. Rod let him know that the business would still run the same way; his homeboy took charge for him.

Tío understood the game—he had been running from a murder charge in L.A for twenty-three years now. He informed Rod that the best way to remain free was to stay out the public eye the most you could.

Rod wasn't sure if the dude he shot had died yet, but he knew the police were looking to question him about it.

After Rod ate lunch with tío, he and Sinfonia headed back to the city of Houston. They went to a Rockets basketball game that night, then to a few clubs.

The girls were all over Rod at the clubs, and Sinfonia didn't like it at *all.* For some reason, all the women thought he was a rapper, but Sinfonia was putting bitches in their place left and right.

Rod thought it was funny and cute how jealous she acted, but they still had a lot of fun and she showed Rod off all week. He even Facetimed Keyshore, Brain, and Roscoe-Cee so they could see all the beautiful friends Sinfonia had, and all his crew promised him they were coming down to hang out soon.

***

Detective V05 called all his officers in for a "Clean Akron Up" meeting. Viv sat in the back of the room as he displayed a photo lineup, but when she saw Zeek's face, she almost spit out the water she was drinking.

Photos of Zeek, Roscoe-Cee, Baby-J, and Rod were all on display. They were considered violent killers that had never been arrested for open murder charges, and they were also active drug dealers.

An outstanding warrant was out for Rod for a shooting, but the victim recanted his statement so all they could do was question him. But he wasn't anywhere to be found, and it was going on two months now.

Detective V05 then posted more sets of photos over top of the ones he already showed. He had photos of Keyshore, Brain, Lil' Mark, and Joy.

He then addressed the meeting.

"These four photos are the top four—we already have the rest of this murderous organization, which reaches all the way from North Dakota to West Virginia. The problem is, we can't get anyone from their group to snitch, and we don't have enough evidence to launch a federal investigation."

Detective V05 shook his head before continuing.

"I want every officer to keep an eye on all these guys, and when patrolling their main areas, which are the Valley of West Akron, and 'down the way' of the East side. It seems to me that the most violent of these sides have formed together a team known as "Murder Bout Money.""

Viv was so overwhelmed as she walked towards the exit door that she didn't even notice that Detective V05 shot her a seductive smile as she left.

She couldn't believe it; they didn't only have Zeek's face, but they also had Miss Brooks' fiancé, Keyshore. Viv was so confused, but Miss Brooks wouldn't rest in peace if she allowed herself not to warn him, at least.

The fact that they really had nothing on them yet made her feel a little better, and she figured telling them to clean their acts up was okay, so Viv called Keyshore first, then Zeek, telling them both the same thing.

Zeek wanted to know who else's faces they had, but she told him nothing and just gave him the warning of a lifetime.

When Keyshore hung up with Viv, his heart dropped—he couldn't believe he was being investigated. But he called everyone from the crew and gave them the ups. He preached that it was nearing the time of the end, and they still needed to purchase close to fifty more houses to at least own the Valley on the West side.

Zeek told Keyshore that Viv told him the same

news, and he felt they had nothing on them, but they all needed to shut down business for a while. In the meantime, they all agreed to meet up in Houston, Texas with Rod.

***

Keyshore was the first one to arrive, then Lil' Mark and Joy, Zeek and Brain, and finally, Roscoe-Cee and Baby-J. The whole team was finally there, and they all managed to sneak out of town without V05 knowing.

Rod felt great—seeing his team in Houston was the best.

Sinfonia and Joy hung out at the stores a lot while Rod and the guys spent a lot of time at the beach and Tío's ranch.

Keyshore loved riding the horses Tio had on his ranch; he couldn't get enough.

But when tío took them on his yacht, their view of living changed forever.

Keyshore shouted, "I told you, Lil' Mark, these yachts are what's up!"

Lil' Mark had to agree, and his mind was set on purchasing himself one soon.

Tío was amazed about how young Baby-J was. The kid was almost fifteen years old in a grown man's body, and he loved everything about Baby-

J's swag—not to mention the murder stories he heard, as well.

Baby-J himself was loving his first experience out of town, so he later sent for Kia and his son to join him.

***

Viv had to smile at herself as she patrolled the West and East sides for weeks without a sign of Keyshore or Zeek. Detective V05 was furious as weeks went by, however, as there wasn't a person on his photo list in sight.

Something was going on, and he wasn't resting until he figured it out.

MURDER BOUT MONEY PART 2

Barrio, lucir, diluvio, de primera clase

CHAPTER 24

Creeping In and Out

Tio's

Brain snuck back into Akron, seeing as he had a shipment coming that contained fifty bricks of coke that he and Rod were responsible for.

The pack wasn't due to land until tomorrow, so he figured he would check his traps and collect all the money that was in the streets.

As he drove through the Valley, he had to smile—the 'hood was starting to look like theirs. It seemed like every house and buildings he drove past, they owned. Things were really coming along... if only they could buy out the new Edgewood projects that had been built.

Brain parked on Lane Street, then entered a trap spot down the street from Rod's mother's house.

He had the young females from the 'hood selling straight coke out the trap—he had learned through his strategic thinking that the business did better than the niggas. As long as he kept his dick out of them, things would continue to run just as smooth.

He counted all the money they had and informed them that the bag would be back in tomorrow. A red-haired Toy made sure that he understood they only had a little under an ounce left, and that tomorrow was the weekend.

Brain reassured her before he left, heading up to Lacroix Street to collect from Rod's little niggas. After he left Lacroix, he went on to Fern Street, Moon Street, and the Murder Block. From there, he headed to the Southwest side, the East side, The Hill, and then back home.

He had all the money rounded up and ready to be sent off to the Mexicans when the shipment came in, but he decided not to visit his baby mom or his other girl while he was in town. He figured it was best if he snuck in and out after he re-supplied everyone else with the product.

When he got home, Brain fell asleep watching Barron's *Finance and Investment* special.

The bricks landed early that next morning. Everything went smooth, and Brain was back in the sky and headed to Houston again by four p.m.

***

Rod was up early, chain-smoking blunts of "Za Za." He had so much on his mind.

He liked Houston, but Akron was his city, and Ohio was his state. He felt homesick; he really was missing the city, and the power his presence made.

Sinfonia rolled over and noticed him smoking blunt after blunt, sitting at the edge of the bed.

"What's wrong, baby?" she asked, sensing the trouble in her man.

Rod shook his head to assure her it was nothing, but they both knew that was a lie, so Sinfonia got up and kissed him on the back as she held him from behind.

"Are you hungry, baby?" she asked as she kissed the back of his neck.

Rod told her he guessed he could go for something to eat, and Sinfonia got up ass-naked and went to the kitchen

The sight of her body made Rod smile to himself—she was truly a beauty, and something one could never get tired of.

Keyshore was up early too—he couldn't get enough of the horses, so he was already at Tío's ranch and taking the black horse he loved for a ride.

Tío looked out the window and smiled to himself. He knew Keyshore was in love with his horses.

After Rod finished his breakfast, he headed over to Tío's to see how the shipment went to Akron. He informed Rod that everything went as planned, and now he was just waiting for the money to make it to him—tío knew it usually took four to five days for the money to come because his truck driver was always the one to drive it back—and Brain was expected back around six p.m., so they seemed to have a great flow going.

Baby-J woke up to Kia sucking his dick, and his eyes popped open soon as he felt her warm tongue go over his dick head.

He looked over at his son, who was still asleep next to him, and then began rubbing Kia's head as she went up and down on his dick.

About fifteen minutes later, Baby-J climaxed all in her mouth, and she swallowed it all.

Once he got himself together again, he got out the bed and walked over to the window, where he could see the beautiful ocean from their condo.

Baby-J was loving the Houston life, and if it was up to him, he *never* wanted to return to the cold streets of Akron.

"It's beautiful, isn't it, babe?" Kia asked as she hugged Baby-J from behind.

"I don't ever want to leave here!" Baby-J said

back to her.

They both stood by the window, looking out for almost an hour before the baby was up and ready for attention.

Zeek woke up with two Mexican women from a night of fun. He had to admit; the love was great in Texas, and the women knew how to party.

He couldn't believe his luck last night at the casino—not only did he win two beautiful women, but he won ninety-thousand on the blackjack table, too.

Lil' Mark and Joy were both up and, on the beach, already with their daughter, Marsha. She was having a ball as she splashed water on the shoreline with her little red bucket and shovel, playing.

Joy packed cold-cuts, chips, sodas, water, fruits, and a bottle of wine and suntan lotion. She and Lil' Mark laid on a large sun blanket, watching Marsha have the time of her life.

Lil' Mark figured he would take a nice swim, so he got up and ran out to the ocean. The water felt great, and he was a great swimmer, so he was comfortable swimming way, deep out. Joy and the baby cheered him on as he continued to swim further, until the waves started to crash over him.

He returned fifteen minutes later, well out of

breath and laughing. He grabbed Marsha up, and he started making her laugh, too.

Roscoe-Cee walked onto the beach and spotted Lil' Mark and Joy with the baby, so he walked over and joined in on the laughter Marsha was giving them.

After talking to them for a while, he decided to go rent a jet-ski and ride in the ocean for a while.

"Life in Houston is a party," he thought as he remembered all the beautiful women he met daily.

Dorinda was coming down next week to hang out with him, and he couldn't wait. Last night he almost let temP.T.ation get the best of him, but he stood loyal to Dorinda.

When Brian landed, he went to see tío, Rod, and Keyshore at the ranch. After they hung out and talked business, he was off to get dressed for a hot date with an Islamic sister he met when he first came.

Brain had to give it to the young sister; she was very spiritual, and looked very nice wearing her hijab. She showed Brain around and introduced him to a few great Muslims. They hung out all that night, and Brain didn't leave from her until two o'clock the next morning.

Everyone ended up in the casino, because Zeek

was on a hot streak. Brain was the last one to arrive; Baby-J and Kia were with Marsha since they were too young to get in.

When Brain got to the blackjack table, Zeek had a twenty-thousand-dollar bet, with twenty showing in his hand. The dealer had thirteen showing, so he had to take a card.

When the dealer flipped over a king of spades, Zeek shouted with approval—he won.

"I'm on fire, Brain!" Zeek shouted, with about a hundred and seventy-five thousand dollars in chips in front of him.

Keyshore and Lil' Mark were at the craps table shooting dice—and they seemed to be losing, Joy and Sinfonia were at the slots, and Rod and Roscoe-Cee were playing poker.

Brain decided he would have a few drinks and cheer his friends on.

By five o'clock that morning, everyone was ready to go.

Except Zeek.

Zeek was still winning big, and Joy was in his ear telling him, "Let's go."

Zeek made his last bet for forty-five thousand—he was already up two-hundred and fifty thousand.

He got dealt a queen of hearts and an eight of spade, so he stayed with the cards he received.

The dealer had a jack of spades and a four of spades showing, so he took a hit.

When his card flipped over, showing an eight of hearts, Zeek jumped up and down.

The crew had to drag Zeek out of the casino—he ended up winning two-hundred and ninety-five thousand dollars. The people at the casino seemed a little upset that his friends pushed him to leave, but they figured he would be back to lose it all.

***

Months came and went—the crew spent over seven months down in Houston before Keyshore decided it was time to go back to Akron.

He was the first to leave, and as the week went on everyone else went on different days.

Rod was the last one to return, mainly because he had to set a conference for him and his lawyers to meet with Detective V05 for questioning about the shooting at the Clutch strip club eight and a half months ago.

As soon as he landed, him and his lawyer met V05 at the police station. Detective V05 knew Rod was responsible, but with the victim changing his statement, he couldn't do much.

He questioned Rod, but Rod's lawyer did all his talking, which led to a half-hour meeting of nothing.

Rod's lawyer shook Detective V05's hand, and just like that, he and Rod left the office. Rod smiled and shook his lawyer's hand once they got outside.

He felt great to be back home, but he informed his lawyer to check his account in a few hours because he had a bonus coming. Rod's lawyer smiled and thanked him as well.

Brain pulled up, Rod jumped in with him, and they both headed to the 'hood.

Sam's corner store was packed as Brain pulled in.

Keyshore was leaning up against a 2022 Benz truck he just purchased, talking to the owner, Sam, and everyone from the crew was outside laughing and talking shit.

Baby-J pulled up in a 2019 Jaguar that was black-on-black with "30 days" tags. He jumped out in all Gucci with the chain Lil' Mark gave him, and a bust-down Rolex watch.

Lil' Mark shouted, "Look at my young boy!" as he smiled in appreciation of Baby-J's growth.

Everyone hugged Rod and shook his hand, happy that he was finished with the shooting situation, and Rod was loving the love as he smoked blunt after blunt.

Everyone knew he would be back, shining hard

by tomorrow—that was just how he was.

The next day, Rod pulled through the 'hood in an all-white-on-white 2022 Range Rover just to let his presence be known.

His 'hood niggas saluted him on every street he turned down, and it felt good to be back home for Rod, where he was a king crowned from birth.

Rod parked his truck on Lacroix and stood outside, smoking blunts with his young niggas as they updated him on all the shit, they couldn't speak over the phone about. Rod listened to all the news and got word that the dude he'd shot was plotting to shoot him back.

Brain wasted no time when he discovered the dude Rod shot was plotting something. He got the drop on the dude the same day Rod told him about him.

He laid in the bushes of the dude's mother's house for hours, and finally, his luck paid off when he pulled in his mother's driveway to grab some drugs he stashed there.

Brain watched as he jumped out of the car and raced inside, and he noticed a female in the front seat and one male in the back.

He shook his head. He couldn't believe the little nigga was riding around without tint on his windows...

Brain pulled his mask down over his face, and as soon as the little nigga came out the door, he rose from the bushes with his AR.

Shots went off, hitting the little nigga in the face, chest, and legs.

He was dead before his body fell off the porch, but the little nigga in the back seat jumped out, shooting towards Brain.

His bullets hit Brain in the arm and chest. Brain fell back, but still managed to hit the other little nigga right between the eyes.

Brain staggered back up to his feet, thanking God that he wore his bulletproof vest. He raced through the back yard of the house next to the victim's, jumped the fence, and got in the rental car he'd driven there.

Blood was dripping down his arm where he was shot, but he didn't want to go to the hospital. Instead, he wrapped a t-shirt around his arm and applied pressure to stop the bleeding.

But his baby's mother ended up taking him to a hospital in Cleveland, where they made a story up.

***

Rod didn't even know that the little nigga he shot got killed, but his lawyer was shouting at the top of his lungs at him. His lawyer couldn't *believe* that Rod allowed such a thing to happen with all that was going on!

After his lawyer finally chilled out some, Rod explained to him that he didn't do it—he didn't even know about the situation until he told him.

"Well, it doesn't look good on your behalf!" his lawyer shouted before hanging up.

Rod shook his head. He couldn't believe his lawyer had the balls to call him and talk to him in such manner.

He made a mental note telling himself it was time to start looking for a new lawyer. All he could think about was as much as he paid him, he should never speak like he did.

When Brain left the hospital in Cleveland, he texted Rod, "Thank me later."

Rod smiled when he received the text—he knew right then and there that Brain took care of the little nigga.

***

Detective V05 pulled onto West Crosier Street, to the house where the victim he had questioned about being shot by Rod laid dead on the porch steps.

Another young kid laid dead by an open car door with a gun still in his hand, and they had the woman who was in the passenger seat when the shooting actually happened in the back of a police car.

The officers quickly updated Detective V05 and informed him that the female witness only saw one person who wore a black ski-mask and all-black clothes. Nobody else saw anything.

The victim's mother was crying in the arms of her boyfriend, and a small crowd of people began to gather around the scene.

Detective V05 hung around until they finally hauled the dead bodies off. He asked the victim's mother a few more questions, and then he left too.

He had a funny feeling that Rod and his crew had something to do with the killings, but the victims seemed to be into it with a lot of different people.

However, his eyes were on Rod and his crew no matter what—they all seemed to pop back up out of the blue after months of disappearance.

This couldn't be a coincidence.

***

Tension was broiling on the East side of Akron.

Zeek was getting a lot of money, and a few of his Blood homies didn't like the fact that he dealt with a group outside the 'hood.

Although they never caught him with Joy, they

knew she was a part of the same group. The fact LX only had the green light on Joy to be murdered was what kept Zeek safe—unless he was caught with her when it went down.

But Zeek's power continued to grow on the East side because of the love he gave and the product he sold for cheap. He also made sure that LX and the rest of his East side Boyz lived well in jail.

Zeek stood outside his car shop, talking to a few of his home Boyz when a green Land Rover pulled up. Two light-skinned dudes with braids in their hair got out dressed all in red.

He knew them from seeing them around in the 'hood, but Zeek had no personal knowledge about them.

The driver introduced himself as "Young B," and his partner said his name was "Fat-B." Zeek shook their hands, gave them the Blood signs, then asked how he could help them.

Zeek almost spit his drink out of his mouth laughing when the fat kid named Fat-B told him that all the East side Bloods had to pay dues to them, but he held his composure just because he was eager to hear why these young niggas felt such a way.

Fat-B continued to explain why, stating that they were building a pot for all the homies to have money in their pockets when they were released from prison.

Zeek was impressed, but there was no way he was paying the little niggas any 'hood taxes. He spoke firmly back and told them that what he would do is front them some drugs and they could save their half and pay his back.

Young B thought about it and then whispered something in Fat-B ear, and they agreed with Zeek's offer.

But what Zeek didn't know was that they had no plans on giving him any money back—period.

Zeek sent one of his young niggas to run and grab a pound of ice for the little Blood homies from the stash, and he stood around smoking a blunt and talking to the Blood homies until his little nigga pulled back up and tossed them a grocery bag with the pound of ice inside.

Zeek told them he only wanted sixty-five hundred, which was cheap for the prices they went for, and both Young B and Fat-B jumped back in the truck after they dapped Zeek up.

After Young B pulled off, Fat-B asked him, "You really don't want to pay him back? He fronted us a pound for dirt-cheap, bro."

He thought about it, and Young B decided that he had to call off not paying Zeek; he figured it would be best if they worked their way up, first. Zeek showed so much love that it was hard to ever want to play him once you got in.

Young B and Fat-B were sixteen years old, but a lot of the homies on the East side had both love and fear for them. They were loyal to the 'hood and the set, and their body count was a fresh high.

Zeek really didn't care or know because he was on a different level now, and he still had no problem with "Murder Bout Money" when it came to business.

To his surprise, Young B and Fat-B came right back the next day with the money and continued to run through a pound every day.

He decided to up them to three pounds, mainly because he didn't like the everyday traffic, but all his workers on the East side didn't like selling shit to them, either.

Young B and Fat-B started really coming up and fucking with Zeek. Although their original plan was to rob him, their love only grew. Zeek was a great dude—none of the O.G.s from the 'hood showed them how to do or believed in them like Zeek did, and they had a gold mine going down in Springfield, Ohio.

Young B had met a white dude named Mickey when he was doing time as a juvenile, and Mickey was everything he said he could be if Young B had an ice connect. All Young B and Fat-B had to do was drive the work to Mickey, and it was gone the same day.

Young B and Fat-B pulled up to Mickey's spot in Springfield, this time with three pounds of ice. When they came in and showed Mickey they brought more, he was very happy.

Mickey looked inside the grocery bag, and quickly started dancing. He wasted no time getting to work. Young B charged him ten thousand for each pound, but Mickey didn't care—he was charging *his* people *thirteen* thousand a pound.

Mickey made a few phone calls, and just like that, they were counting and splitting the money up. Young B and Fat-B were loving the easy situation, and they had to ask Mickey how much he could move in a day.

Mickey told them he believed he could run through at least ten pounds a week, and dollar signs lit up in Young B and Fat-B's heads. The only problem was that they didn't want Zeek to know where they were getting money at, but with the way it was going, they just had to.

When Young B and Fat-B pulled back to Akron and called Zeek to give him his money, Zeek couldn't believe it.

He met them on 5th Avenue at his old house, and when they pulled up, Zeek was in a rental car with a beautiful, foreign-looking chick. Zeek passed her the blunt, then got out to talk with the young homies, signaling for them to follow him inside.

When they got inside, Fat-B tossed him the bag with the money they owed him.

Zeek looked inside and shook his head, asking them, "How you selling the product so fast?"

Young B took a long pause and then told him, "That's what we needed to talk to you about."

Zeek told them to take a seat and began rolling a blunt. After he finished rolling the blunt, he lit it and told Young B to inform him on what was going on.

Young B told him about his white friend, Mickey, down in Springfield, Ohio and how all they do was give it to him, he'd make a few calls, and everything would be gone.

Zeek passed Fat-B the blunt as he asked, "How much do you think your white friend can move?"

Young B told Zeek what Mickey told him, which was about ten pounds a week.

Zeek nodded his head, and then asked Young B, since he always seemed to be driving, "Do you have license? Whose truck you driving?"

Young B told him that he didn't have license, but the truck belonged to an older girl he was fucking. Zeek couldn't believe they were brave enough to take a chance on the highway like that, but he respected the hustler in them.

Zeek looked them in the eyes, and he told them he would fund them the ten pounds.

Fat-B shouted excitedly, “Yes!”

He also told them that he would provide them a licensed driver and that they wouldn’t be driving that truck back down there.

The next day, Zeek put the ten pounds of ice in a fake gas tank hooked to the black truck he sent them in, and he had a white lady friend drive them since she could pass for being the young homies’ mother.

He also sent her to rent an apartment for them so they would always have their own spot.

CHAPTER 25

Mr. 3/28/77
Shuffle Up and Deal

Rod had Tío on speaker phone while Keyshore, Lil' Mark, Brain, Joy, Roscoe-Cee, Zeek, and Baby-J all sat in his man cave in the basement.

They all were tipsy and high off some good weed, and money was everywhere from the tables to three trash bags.

Rod shouted over the phone to tío, "How much does seven million in hundred-dollar bills weigh?"

Tio laughed out loud back, then said, "It tips the scale at a hundred and fifty pounds!"

Everybody looked at Rod since he had just weighed the shit, and he nodded his head 'yep.'

Tío shouted, "Don't get silent, motherfucker!" and everyone busted out laughing hard.

Keyshore jumped in, instigating, "What, you thought tío got all that shit he got for free?"

Rod shot Keyshore a "fuck you, nigga" look and

told tío he was seeing how sharp his math was.

Tío was in full form now, and he was feeling himself—he told Rod he didn't even count his money anymore; he just buys what he wants. They all shared a few more laughs with tío before Rod rushed him off the phone.

When Rod hung up, Brain asked him, "Why you ask that rich-ass Mexican a question like that?"

Rod laughed and had to agree—tío was true motivation! Their whole team together wasn't worth even close to half of Tío's eighteen-year-old son.

It took Keyshore and his crew almost twenty-four hours to count all the money they had together. After they finished, every dollar was divided accurately.

It was no secret that the Mexican plugs made the most. Business was good, though, and Keyshore loved the fact that his crew all bought houses and businesses in the 'hood.

Meeting Tío really changed a lot in Keyshore; the Mexican plug he and Lil' Mark had before him never talked or hung out with them. Tío really put a higher standard on Keyshore's mind.

Keyshore was back, and in rare form, he opened a new trap on Fern Street; the trip to Houston had really put his mind on a higher level.

He had a few of his old-school dudes around, even though he knew they got high, but one thing Keyshore learned was that no matter a person's status, you could always learn something new.

As Keyshore parked on the curve, old-school Terry Lee and Monkey Shine walked up from off the porch. Keyshore dapped them up and listened as Terry Lee went to work running some game.

Terry Lee made sure Keyshore walked all around the house as he showed him the great work, they had done cleaning the yard, and Keyshore handed them both fifty dollars after he inspected their work.

Once they made it inside, Keyshore showed them all the rooms he needed painted and cleaned out.

Terry Lee and Monkey Shine went straight to work, and Keyshore sat on the porch while his old-school homies worked inside the house.

It was a beautiful day; a few customers even pulled up and bought some grams of Feddy. Keyshore had grams that went to a thousand, but he also had grams that took five, ten, twenty, forty, and fifty. He wasn't turning down any bread—the only room he left was for his team to eat, and they had all the junkies pulling up, too.

After his dude from Mansfield, Ohio pulled off, Keyshore went back into the house to see if his old-school homies wanted anything from the store. He already figured they would want some beer, and they confirmed his thoughts.

Keyshore decided he would walk to Sam's store this time, since it was only down the street from his new trap. He reached into his truck and grabbed his .357 revolver, then placed it in between his hip and belt.

As he walked down V. Odom Boulevard, cars blew at him, and once he got by the barbershop, he noticed Lil' Mark inside getting a haircut. Keyshore decided to walk in and gave everybody some love, then told Lil' Mark to pull up on Fern when he was finished.

When Keyshore got to Sam's store, he ran into Baby-J, who must have been selling crack and ice to five different people.

He shook his head and went inside the store to get some beer and single cigarettes.

As he was paying for his items, Baby-J came in, talking shit. They dapped each other, then hugged, and Baby-J laughed when he seen the lady hand Keyshore six single cigarettes.

"Why don't you just buy a pack?" Baby-J asked in between laughs.

He then pulled out a knot of money and told the lady to give him a pack of *Newport 100*s in a box. Baby-J handed Keyshore the pack, shaking his head.

Keyshore laughed because he knew Baby-J

was being funny, but he didn't hesitate to acceP.T. the cigarettes.

They walked out of the store together, and Keyshore noticed Baby-J had a few little girls in his car. Baby-J caught his eye and knew what he was thinking before he even said anything.

Baby-J told him Kia was home with the baby, and Keyshore could do nothing but shake his head.

"Why you tint your windows if you going to allow people to be in your car with the windows rolled down?"

He had a point, so Baby-J shouted over to the girls in his car to roll his windows up.

Keyshore stood in front of the store talking to Baby-J for a few more minutes, then he headed back to his trap.

Lil' Mark pulled up a half hour later.

They smoked a few blunts and went over a few business numbers, and Keyshore made sure he understood that they were turning their hustle up more. He also told Lil' Mark that they needed to break some of the big grams down and trap them out.

Lil' Mark decided it was best for Keyshore to handle the Feddy, and he and Joy would work the ice fully.

Keyshore found himself living in the trap. He

hustled 24/7 out of the house on Fern Street. Business was booming; he had niggas coming from all over Ohio to buy grams.

He kept Terry Lee and Monkey Shine around him a lot. He didn't care what they did—they kept him sharp and down to earth.

He and Brain stopped doing their meetings. Keyshore's only focus was making money. He wasn't even getting pussy that much, his mind being so determined on having all the millions that they paid the plugs.

To the people in the 'hood, they were rich, but on the level tío and the other Mexican plugs were, they were nothing. Even though they owned most of the 'hood that they lived in, Keyshore still felt the money needed to grow a *lot* more.

Terry Lee asked Keyshore, "Why you still taking chances with the game?"

He couldn't understand what more Keyshore wanted. He watched Keyshore count thousands of dollars every day, and that was just from the short time he hustled on Fern Street.

Keyshore took a long pause, and then he told Terry Lee, "I am trying to own the whole 'hood and create jobs for my people in the community."

Terry Lee shook his head.

He told Keyshore, "It already looks like y'all own the 'hood. You chasing a game that has a never-ending story, youngster—you'll never have enough money when you selling drugs to get it. The game is never-ending. It's been like that before you and will be *after* you. The smartest thing you can do is get out as a winner—trust me."

Keyshore understood, but still he had his own reasons, and he wasn't getting out until he met them.

Monkey Shine told Keyshore, "You should really take Terry Lee's advice."

He told Keyshore how they once were major players and hustlers in the same 'hood he called his own. He went on to explain that the game caught up with them because they weren't smart enough to leave as winners.

***

Keyshore woke up in the trap at around five o'clock in the morning. He checked his phone, and seeing he had a few missed calls, he quickly called back.

Minutes later, people were already coming and leaving with their product.

He looked in the refrigerator, despite knowing there wasn't shit in it to eat. The sight of a few half-full beer bottles, a few bottled waters, and an old box of pizza made him laugh as he shut the refrigerator again.

Keyshore gathered up all the money he made, then filled his book bag up with it. After that, he hid the rest of the drugs he had left and left the trap.

The whole day, the wise words Keyshore's old-school homies had given to him ate at him. He felt like he was having a reality check, but there were two sides—and the other side was telling him, "Fuck that! Get all the money you can get while the getting is good."

Keyshore thought he needed to do a little shopping, so he headed to Summit Mall to ease his mind. He bought himself a few outfits and a couple pairs of shoes, and after a few hours shopping, he decided to go down to the food court in the mall to grab a bite to eat.

As he stood in line waiting to order, he noticed a beautiful dark brown woman staring at him. He smiled at her, and she returned a smile of her own.

Keyshore ordered himself a Philly cheesesteak sandwich, a small order of fries, and a large cup of pink lemonade with strawberries in it. Once he received his order, he sat by himself and enjoyed his lunch.

After he finished eating, he grabbed his bags and left the mall.

As he was putting his items in his trunk, the dark-brown-skinned woman approached him.

She told him that she didn't usually do this type of stuff, but her heart wouldn't allow her to let him get away without knowing who he was.

Keyshore smiled. He was flattered by the woman's bold attemP.T., but he was also smart about meeting new people.

He looked her in the eyes, and he could sense the sincerity in her, but still told her his name was "Kay."

She introduced herself, stating her name was "Sissy."

They exchanged phone numbers and made plans to hook up later. Keyshore pulled off, thinking to himself how he barely got any pussy since his fiancé, Miss Brooks, died from Covid-19.

He shook his head and turned up his music when NBA Young Boy came on. Keyshore had to give the nigga NBA his props; the young nigga's music was really good to him.

Meanwhile, across town on the East side, Young B and Fat-B had it going on. Young B bought himself a 2019 SRT truck, and Fat-B bought a 2018 SRT charger.

They were killing them down in Springfield, Ohio, and niggas in Akron didn't have a clue.

Zeek made it a dream come true, and the respect was all for him.

Fat-B pulled up on Kia when he noticed her

getting gas. He always wanted to fuck her, but Baby-J ended up getting to her first and having a child with her. Fat-B didn't care about Baby-J—they knew each other, but Baby-J was from the Valley's West side.

When Kia reached to grab the pump, Fat-B jumped out of his car and told her, "Let me pump that for you, beautiful."

She smiled and allowed Fat-B to pump her gas, and she had to admit; he was looking really nice.

After Fat-B finished, she thanked him, then got into her car. Fat-B walked up to her window and asked if he could take her to dinner one day.

Kia was flattered, but she couldn't—Baby-J would kill them both, so she told Fat-B that it wouldn't be a great idea because she was still with her son's dad.

Fat-B told her to still take his number, just in case she changed her mind.

Kia took his number, but when he left, she quickly erased it. She wasn't taking that type of chance.

Young B was at the park shooting dice when Fat-B pulled up. The park was packed with East side niggas, so Fat-B left his gun in the car. When he walked up, Young B was on the dice with a fist full of money in his hand.

Young B shouted, "You better get some of this sweet money, Fat-B!" then continued shooting the dice for his point.

After the second roll, Young B watched as the dice stopped rolling, showing his point; eight.

Young B shouted, “Don’t nobody move but the money!” as he raked up all his money.

As he finished picking up the money, police suddenly swarmed the park from everywhere.

Niggas started running, tossing drugs and guns everywhere. The police got at least twenty of them laid out on the ground and they took thirteen thousand from Young B.

Of course, he was furious, but he was glad he didn’t have his gun or drugs on him.

After the police finished searching everyone, they allowed the ones who had nothing on them to leave.

Fat-B told Young B that he wasn’t getting in his car because he left his gun in it. Young B laughed and told him he had done the same, so they decided to walk to the drive thru on the Lane.

The big homie “Eighteen” had the good smoke, so Fat-B bought a few grams for them to smoke until shit cooled down.

While they stood in front of the drive thru smoking, Baby-J drove past, looking hard.

Fat-B smiled at Baby-J, then told Young B, “I’m at that nigga’s bitch; I’m going to give him a reason to mean-mug.”

They dapped each other, then laughed at the

whole situation.

After things cooled off later that night, Young B and Fat-B made it back to their vehicles. Fat-B had a hot date with a girl from Joy Park apartments, so he headed straight to the liquor store.

Young B was more laid back now that he understood the level to the game and getting money, so he headed to his older lady friend's house to chill. She had his back when he was down, and he felt it was only right to surround himself with a woman that was truly for him.

***

Zeek had to admit; things were going great for him. He was seeing the most money he ever had in his life.

Joy pulled up to Zeek's trap on 5th Avenue—it had been forever since she'd been there, or even on the East side *period.*

When she parked and got out, Zeek was standing on the porch with his gun in his hand.

She smiled. She had so much love and respect for Zeek—she knew he would die or kill for her without question.

Joy walked up on the porch and hugged Zeek before they went inside and handled their business.

After Joy counted all the money from the book bag, she put it back in, then strapped it around her arms and on her back.

Zeek ran to her car to grab the two duffel bags full of pounds of ice, and when he returned, he walked her to her car and watched as she pulled off. Once Joy was safely enroute, he went back in the trap to count the pounds.

Everything went smooth, and Joy texted him when she made it home safe. Zeek couldn't believe how Young B and Fat-B were still running through the pounds, but he sure was glad.

Tomorrow, he decided, he would send twenty pounds instead of the ten that he always sent. He texted his driver and told her to be over early so that by the time his little homies came, shit would be ready to go straight to Springfield, Ohio.

By the time Young B and Fat-B made it to the trap, Zeek had everything ready and loaded. They jumped in with the older white woman, and off they went.

Once they made it there safely, his driver texted to let him know.

Zeek was in a great money flow—everyone around him was eating and playing their position, so he headed to the West side to fuck with Keyshore on Fern Street.

When he pulled up, Keyshore was sitting on the porch with the old heads. Zeek jumped out from the rental car he was driving and noticed that Keyshore and the two old heads all had pistols in their hands.

Keyshore smiled once he realized it was Zeek.

"Boooy! You almost got shot, jumping out fast like that!" Keyshore shouted as they all put their guns back on their hips.

Zeek dapped everyone up, then sat on the porch with them.

"Damn, Keyshore, you even got the grandpas strapped, I see," Zeek said with a serious face.

"We all one over here," Keyshore explained, "They taught me the game for real—and still do."

Terry Lee took over the conversation from there. He was giving lessons on structure and the importance of a foundation. With the way things were going, Zeek needed this conversation, so he listened carefully.

One thing he loved about Keyshore was the way he treated everyone equally, and now he was learning the importance of why.

Terry Lee went on to explain how important it was to always make the people around you as strong as you, and how important it is to hear out everyone in your circle's ideas and suggestions.

"Never react off impulse," he said, "this is a thinking man's game, what we call life; all the super hard and tough guys always seem to die fast, because they couldn't think before they reacted."

CHAPTER 26

The Famed Promise of Death, or Life in Jail

Goldie and Skelton's murder trial had the whole city of Akron tuned in.

Skelton had already received twenty years in the feds from the conspiracy charge he caught in North Dakota, so when the verdict came back "not guilty" for murder, the court room eruP.T.ed with cheers.

But right after the cheers, the family of the victims eruP.T.ed in violence, throwing chairs, and storming towards the judge's bench. People were fighting everywhere, and Goldie and Skelton were hauled off quickly by officers.

Goldie was later sentenced to fifteen years for the charges he caught when the task force raided, looking for him.

Keyshore and Brain felt a little better knowing that their young niggas would see the light again. Goldie was in the State, so a little money could get him home in ten. Skelton, on the other hand would do at least sixteen years out of that twenty.

Keyshore got up off his La-Z-Boy chair and walked over to his fish tank to feed his baby sharks while Brain poured himself another shot from Keyshore's bar. He drank it down in one gulp, then chased it with a bottle of water.

"This place really looks nice," Brain said.

Keyshore had everything redone since Miss Brooks passed—he figured it was the only way he would ever work himself back to normal. The loss of her was still killing him, and it was going on two years since she died.

He looked over towards Brain and told him that he spent close to ninety thousand redecorating the whole house. Keyshore had to hold back his tears, because no matter what he did, his heart wouldn't let him stop thinking about Miss Brooks.

Brain caught the look and hurt in Keyshore eyes, so he quickly changed the subject.

Brain had a plan, and he wanted to make sure his big homie had first pick and choice. He began telling Keyshore about a hick town in Erie, Pennsylvania that he stumbled on. He told Keyshore about how they paid top dollar for the coke he had, and how lately, they been asking for some Feddy and ice.

When he told Keyshore the prices he'd told

them, Keyshore couldn't believe it. Since shit got shut down in North Dakota, Keyshore hadn't seen or heard anything else so sweet until now.

Since Lil' Mark was handling all the ice, Keyshore told Brain he would have to cut him in on the ice.

As Brain continued to give Keyshore the rundown, it was like music to his ears.

Brain left Keyshore's house close to two o'clock in the morning, since he had a nigga short-stopping one of his trap spots on the Southwest side. He already checked the nigga once, and he figured the nigga was only doing it because he had a female running the spot.

Brain parked his car on South Street and walked up Victory Street towards the trap. He was in all black, and as he approached the house, he caught the nigga in the driveway selling to one of the customers.

As soon as the little nigga stuck his head from back out the customer's car window, Brain shot him right in the face.

The customer quickly pulled off when she saw the first shot, but Brain walked up on him and emptied the whole clip in him.

Without a care in the world, he turned around, walked back to his car, and drove off. He called his female worker and told her to shut down for the night, which she already knew from the dead body in the yard next to her trap.

Brain cussed himself out though when he realized he didn't take the money or drugs from the little nigga he just killed.

Keyshore was up early the next morning, but he couldn't figure why since he sleP.T. most of his nights in the trap.

He laid in his king-sized bed, daydreaming for about fifteen minutes before he got up, brushed his teeth, and jumped in the shower.

After he got out of the shower, he got dressed, and then he cooked himself breakfast.

The moment he turned his cellphones on, they began to ring nonstop. He had money coming from everywhere as he told each customer to meet him on Fern Street, and by the time he made it to the trap, there were close to twenty-five cars lined up waiting for him.

Terry Lee and Monkey Shine were sitting on the porch, and before Keyshore even got out of his car, they stood in front of him with their guns in hand.

Keyshore went into the trap to grab his bag, then one by one, he served every customer in their cars.

After all the traffic died down, they broke out the chessboard and began playing chess.

Keyshore wasn't a match for either of his old-school homies, but he still played.

***

Young B and Fat-B were back again from their trip out of town.

Zeek counted the money while they rolled blunts and passed them in rotation. He had to admit; his young homies had a great movement going. Every dollar they owed was there, and they never came short. Shit got so real that even Lil' Mark and Joy wanted to meet the young Boyz that Zeek bragged about.

He knew Joy couldn't meet them because of the bad blood she had in their set, but Lil' Mark wasn't a problem.

After the little homies left, Zeek called Joy to meet up, but she was out with her daughter, so he just took all the money he made from his little niggas and the rest of his customers to the safe house.

When he left the safe house, he decided to head to the West side to fuck with Baby-J on the Murder Block.

Baby-J was standing on the porch when he parked and got out, and he really had the block jumping as customers came and went. His young niggas sold everything from clothes, to guns, cars, and drugs.

Zeek loved fucking with Baby-J—there was something about him that attracted him to the young nigga.

Baby-J gave Z dap soon as he walked up on the porch, and Zeek fired up a few blunts as they talked for about an hour and a half.

But as Zeek got up to leave, black trucks surrounded from every direction.

He couldn't believe his eyes; the feds were hitting the block.

Niggas were running everywhere, and they rushed Baby-J and Zeek on the porch. When they searched them, they both had handguns on them, and inside the house they found more guns and drugs.

The fucked-up part about everything was that Zeek was the only grown adult—everyone else was under eighteen years old. The feds had buys from Baby-J and a few of his crew members, but when they learned their ages, they knew they were in for a long day.

Once they discovered who Zeek was, they sent feds to search his two houses, but luckily, they found nothing. Zeek was still pissed as they booked him into Summit County jail later that night, but it was a good thing his gun was made in Ohio, and he never sold to any undercovers.

Baby-J and ten of his crew members were

booked into Dan Street Juvenile Hall, and Zeek was all over the news and in the newspapers, but the fact remained the same; they could only charge him for the gun they found on him. They did, however, confiscate over forty-thousand in cash, eighty-thousand dollars' worth of drugs in street value, fifteen weapons, and some boxes of ammunition.

Joy had a lawyer in court and on Zeek's case that next morning. He bonded out, but he was forced to wear a GPS system on his leg. Although the feds couldn't get him, they were still on his ass.

Baby-J and his crew, however, were into it with the young East side Blood niggas early that next morning in Dan Street. When one of the Blood's Boyz tossed milk on Baby-J, all hell broke out.

Baby-J stabbed the dude in the eye with his spoon, and it was a fully-fledged Bloods vs. Crips riot in seconds. Baby-J and his crew were well advanced and came out victorious in the riot, but everyone that fought was either put in the box or their cell for two weeks straight.

When Keyshore got the news about Zeek and Baby-J, he was sick with worry, but glad that Zeek didn't go fed and Baby-J was still a kid. Since the sweep happened right around the corner from his trap on Fern Street, he quickly shut down and got the fuck out of the V.

Word got back that someone in the 'hood was telling, and Brain was on it like white on rice. When he found out Baby-J's ex-bitch dropped a dime on him, his heart filled with anger and murder.

But as bad as he wanted to do the job, Joy ended up doing it, leaving the young lady, her sister, and her mother dead in a burnt-down house.

***

Lil' Mark pulled up to the new barbershop on V. Odom and Hawkins, but when he walked in and saw all the pics of the dead niggas from his 'hood, there was no way he could stay or get a haircut.

The shit made him very sad, and he thought whoever came up with the idea was stupid.

He walked right back out and headed to the barbershop at the bottom of V. Odom where the gangsters roamed, instead.

Roscoe-Cee pulled up to Brain's trap on Lane Street. Life was getting food back for him all week.

Brain had ten pounds of "Za Za" he took from a nigga a week ago, and he told Roscoe-Cee he could get them for twenty-five hundred a pound if he purchased them all.

When Roscoe-Cee entered the trap, he was amazed at how Brain had beautiful women everywhere.

Brain took him into the basement and sold him the pounds, and on the way back up, he noticed one of the beautiful women selling a customer some coke. Roscoe-Cee looked over at Brain but didn't say anything as he walked out of the trap with a book bag full of pounds of weed.

Life in the ghetto never seemed to change; money being made, life being cheated, blacks going to jail, kids being taught wrong... Roscoe-Cee promised himself that he would never allow himself to get tangled back in deep—weed was the only thing he would ever sell again.

***

Weeks had gone by since the feds snatched Baby-J and his crew. Kia felt so alone without her baby father, but her cousin finally got her to get out the house.

They hit the clubs downtown, then a few bars on the East side. It was close to one-thirty in the morning when they came out from their breakfast spot and headed home.

Fat-B pulled up as they came out, and when he saw Kia, he put the rental truck he was driving in park. He jumped out, designer-down with a big chain on his neck and bust-down Rolex watch with diamonds everywhere and wasted no time talking to Kia.

Her cousin was really checking him out.

Fat-B knew Baby-J was locked up, but he played it like he didn't. He convinced Kia and her cousin to come to an after-hours that his oldie homie owned. Kia really didn't want to go, but her cousin did, so she went along.

Fat-B had his charm on. He purchased all the drinks and smoked blunt after blunt with them, and when it was time to go, he gave Kia his number again and she promised him she would use it.

He also talked Young B out of the house, and he knocked off Kia's cousin. But Fat-B really had Kia's attention, and she was sure to hook back up with him if he called.

Fat-B and Kia started seeing each other every day. It started off as friendly dates but ended up sexually. Although it wasn't supposed to be nothing more than creeping, Kia started catching feelings.

Fat-B took right off where Baby-J left; he made sure Kia and her son had the best. When she became pregnant by him, he moved her and her son to Springfield, Ohio. With her living there, it made it easier for them both—they no longer had to sneak around.

The house he rented for them was beautiful, and Kia decorated it from the top to bottom. Kia knew she was playing with fire, but it was too late—she was in too deep to turn back.

Young B was happy for his boy, but he also felt that Fat-B wasn't thinking the situation all the way through. He knew Baby-J was dangerous, and it was only a matter of time before word got to him.

When Kia had the gender reveal party for her baby and Zeek showed up for Fat-B, she almost choked on the bottled water she was drinking.

Zeek couldn't believe his eyes when Fat-B introduced Kia to him as his first child's mother. He shook her hand quietly and gave her congrats, deciding to let it play out, but he made a mental note to do some investigating later.

When it came time for the reveal, Kia and Fat-B jumped with joy when the blank in the gun shot out pink smoke.

"It's a girl!" Kia screamed as she jumped up and down.

***

Zeek couldn't stop thinking about Kia being Fat-B's baby's mother. His first-time visiting

Springfield, Ohio brought chills to him. Baby-J was damn-near his little brother, and he knew he had to update him.

His lawyer had worked his ass off to get the GPS off his ankle and he only had four months before he turned himself in to do eighteen months for the gun charge. This was his first day being off GPS, and already a lot was going on.

Zeek shook his head.

He wasn't going to the stress about it—shit, there was so many fine women at the gender reveal party that he figured he might as well try to get him some new pussy.

CHAPTER 27

Came in the Game with No Name, Just a Strap

Roscoe-Cee was back on top where he belonged, but he never saw it coming as he dropped his children back off at his baby's mother's.

She walked right up to the car and shot him in the face four times, then killed the kids. When the police got to the crime scene, she was found in the bathroom with a bullet in her head.

Seeing the children laid out dead was hard for everyone—even the police officers.

When word got back to Brain, he cried like a baby. He couldn't believe Roscoe-Cee died in such a manner.

Keyshore was crushed when word got to him, too—but he had lost so much that he couldn't cry anymore. Everyone he loved or cared deeply about seemed to die or get killed. So, he just sat in his house and got really drunk, until he passed out.

***

When it rains, it pours.

Lil' Mark and Joy's daughter was becoming sick. She died from cancer two weeks later, and there was nothing the doctors could do to save her.

Joy felt the weight of the world on her shoulders for the second time in her life.

This time, the pain was unhealing. Rage and hurt overpowered her mind and her thinking. The killer was back in her—she felt no love or feelings. Lil' Mark wasn't himself either, and they both began to do a lot of X-pills and drank Lean.

Baby-J was sentenced to Juvenile life, and he was lucky to dodge the Feds. The only reason they let him slide was because his record wasn't bad, and he was only fifteen years old, going on sixteen.

The crazy part about it all was that everyone else was even younger than him, but Baby-J's lawyer managed to work out a deal with the courts to allow Baby-J out at eighteen instead of twenty-one if he got his GED and stayed out of trouble.

When Fat-B and Little B got in town a week after the baby shower, Zeek met with them at the trap. It was eating him up knowing that Fat-B and Kia had a baby. Every time he thought about saying something to Fat-B, his heart wouldn't allow him.

The game was the game, and Baby-J would have to respect the situation and move on. Besides, Fat-B owed Baby-J no loyalty.

After the money was all counted, Zeek smoked a few more blunts with them, and everyone went their own way. The game was "Murder Bout Money;" not pussy.

Keyshore was up and back to business. He had just purchased two more houses in the 'hood. Skelton sold them to him because he didn't want to invest any more money into fixing the houses he didn't already have finished. With him being in the feds, Skelton felt it would be best to sell and rent to keep his money coming.

But Keyshore started to really worry about Lil' Mark and Joy. They weren't the same, and he honestly understood and felt their pain, but what really bothered him was how they popped X pills and drank lean all day every day since the baby died.

He didn't even know if Lil' Mark was keeping up with the counts and the business they had going with the ice.

Joy pulled up to the trap on 5th Avenue to drop off forty pounds of ice for Zeek and grab the money he owed her.

When she entered the house, Zeek hugged her tight. He could still see and feel the pain in Joy's heart.

They talked for about an hour before she left with the book bag full of money, and Zeek walked her to her car like he always did after they did big business. He told Joy he loved her, and she made promises to have breakfast with him tomorrow.

But when Joy turned off 5th Avenue by Rocky's corner store, Fat-B ran up on her car, shooting her in the head and chest.

When she ran into the curve, he raced up to her car, pushed her dead body to the passenger side, and pulled off.

Zeek's heart went into panic mode when he heard the gunshots. He quickly called Joy's phone to make sure she was safe, but he got no answer.

Fat-B couldn't believe his luck when he opened the book bag and saw all of the bands, and he had been doing his homework on Joy for almost a year and a half!

When he thought he dropped his phone in

Zeek's trap one time, he stumbled on a car, and he had followed Joy in it. His luck paid off, and she fell right in his lap.

He burnt her and the car up, but decided it was best he kept the murder and robbery to himself.

When Zeek pulled up to the corner of 5th Avenue, everything looked the same. There wasn't any sign of a shooting, or people gathered around, but he sent Joy a text telling her to make sure she called him when she got home.

Zeek knew his days on the street were coming to an end; soon, he would be in prison for the gun charge he caught.

To be continued.

FIRST CLASS HUSTLER PUT IN THE BAG

To win, it takes strength, dedication, chancing, loyalty, sacrificing, leadership, direction-following, heart, and most of all, God.

It doesn't matter your worth in wealth, because when you die, you can't take the money with you. But what *does* matter is your relationship with God, your character, and morals as a person, and how you were for your family and loved ones.

Live for the day, but always pray to see tomorrow, thank God every chance you get, smile a lot, love a lot, don't waste your time being mad, and forgive but never forget.

It's not about color; it's about *respect*, honestly. We all must learn that in order for the world to be a better place, God is the only judge.

Remember that even when all goes wrong, have faith.

ABOUT THE AUTHOR

I come from a rare breed, and my life has been a true testimony. I would like to first thank God, and everyone that supports me, family friends etc.. it's too many to name I appreciate all the love.

To my son Little JLAB I know you're watching over your dad, I won't fail you! The street life is only a steppingstone. To all my people that's still stuck in it, you to have a plan to make a way for your family, family is very important. At the end of the day, you are your own destiny. Put God first and thank him every day. Writing is a passion I write a variety of different types of books from Urban Literature, Inspirational, Self-improvement. A percentage of all profits from my book sales will go towards kids fighting cancer, and people wrongly convicted and those over sentenced no matter color or race. I'm a God loving man that believes we are all one like God teaches.

Yours Truly J.LAB

Coming Soon

JAQUAR LATIMER
THE
C.O CONNECT
PARENTAL ADVISORY EXPLICIT CONTENT
PUT IT IN THE BAG PUBLISHING

Coming Soon

My Life Still In Chains
Memoir By: Jaquar Latimer
Put It In The Bag Publishing

Made in the USA
Middletown, DE
12 June 2022

66893606R00166